Waiting for the Perfect Man

By Delena Kay Flakes

www.ragenterprise.com

*A*ngela is a young woman, waiting on the man she hopes and believes she will marry. While she is waiting, she has distractions to overcome. On the one hand, she has the man who is willing to give her the world on a string. On the other hand, there is Kenneth, the man of her dreams. Follow her story through this entanglement of love, trust, hatred, deceit, lust, and desperation as Angela struggles to wait on God for her perfect man!

What others are saying

This book has touched every one of my emotions! I have cried, felt fear, anger, love, excitement, hope, and I have laughed until I fell out of my seat! This is a must read book!--**C. Brown**

The writer has successfully written this book in such a way that almost anyone can relate to the characters. There is something in this book that will touch anyone who reads it.--**F. McDaniel**

The writer has given us a book that is entertaining and humorous, yet, at the same time, inspirational and spiritually based.--**S. Abbage**

I laughed until I cried, then I laughed and cried some more! Every woman should read this book. You will be glad you did!—**D. Ellis**

Everyone who reads this book will be able to see a glimpse of themselves. Either where you are or where you want to be. I have been encouraged. I know God has a blessing just for me!—**H. Griffin**

ACKNOWLEDGEMENTS

To God, my heavenly Father, thank You for allowing the gifts You have given me, to be used in this manner. Let these words and these stories speak to the spirit of the reader as to cause them to love more and to expect more love.

To my husband, thank you for loving me the way you do. No, neither of us is perfect, per se, but we both believe we are perfect for each other. I thank God for you. I love you. Your love for me inspires me.

To my Mother, you always encourage me to do the things I believe I can do, no matter what those things are. Thank you for your strength, for you have strengthened me.

Thank you my sisters, my brother and my children, you all are my favorite cheerleaders!

Thanks to my friends who have laughed and cried with me through this project.

Thanks to my Dad for your faith in me. Thank you for helping me to make my dream come true.

FOREWORD

This is a Christian Romance Story. Even in the lives of Christians, we are faced with the same emotions, the same problems, the same desires as the rest of the world. Constantly, we have to decide between what we want and what God wants for us. Christians have the same desires and physical needs as anyone else. We constantly have to "crucify our flesh" in order to live holy lives for Jesus Christ.

The purpose of this story is to bring forth our meager attempt to deal with our desires and passions, while, at the same time, seeking God's will in our lives. Yes, it is a fight, it is a struggle but in the end, if we remain faithful to God, He remains faithful to us in all that we do.

Additionally, this story causes us to look at some of the issues in our own lives, as women, wives, girl-friends trying to find a husband, young women, single mothers, business/professional women, and women of virtue. It is the hope of this writer to touch on some of the "soft spots" in our lives and shed light on the dark places so that we can began to deal with them face to face. I am a firm believer that the first step to solving a problem is admitting that you have one.

Although this book has been inspired by actual events in my life, this book is so fictionalized and is such an exaggeration of life that the truth is hardly recognizable. If there are any similarities to anyone, it is merely coincidental.

Some of the actual events in my life are: my husband brought a single rose to me at a beauty shop; he had one single, lavender rose delivered to my place of employment for our anniversary; our wedding colors were lavender and white; I really, *really* hate white boxers. The way my husband and I met and the way we were reunited, favor the stories in the book. I really have a keep sake box with all of the letters and cards my husband has given to me over the years of our relationship. He still has all of the letters I've sent him. My husband still kisses me on the base of my neck, right where my neck and shoulders meet. For the many other things that my husband and I have shared, continue to read my books.

It was my goal to touch as many women's lives as possible with the writing of this book. My ministerial calling is for women who are hurting. Even in today's modern society, women are still being placed on the back burner and are often considered as less than desirable in this male dominated society. Even still, our desire as women is to love and be loved. I pray that you will be entertained, but even more importantly, encouraged and inspired.

Chapter 1

DEIDRE'S BEAUTY SALON & BARBER SHOP

Deirdre's Beauty Salon and Barber Shop is where I found myself every Saturday morning. Even when I wasn't getting my hair done, I would go by the shop to speak to Ms. Dee, (as we all called her) meet up and talk with friends, and just to "hang out" on Saturday mornings.

Ms. Dee and her husband own the building where the beauty shop was located. The building contained not only the barber shop and beauty salon, but right next door, there was a nail salon. At the end of the building, there was Ms. Dee's boutique, RAG Design and Apparel. Ms. Dee and her husband were successful entrepreneurs. Their businesses in the neighborhood convinced many other African-American in this area that they could be successful.

My story takes place mostly at the beauty salon and barber shop, so let me talk about that more. Inside the shop, the first station or first area consisted of 5 barber chairs. They were lined up on the same side as the entrance door. Directly in front of the barber chairs, on the opposite side of the room, was the hair dryers' room. It was enclosed with a waist high wall and tinted glass. Women could sit in the hair dryer area and observe the men as they entered into the shop, on the barber's side.

We would sit in the dryer room and make comments about the men as they came in. We enjoyed our autonomy. We could see them, but they couldn't see us. You can imagine how many times we sat in that dryer room, identifying our "baby's daddy"!

The rear of the shop is where the hairstylist chairs and shampoo bowls were located. In addition to that, was an office space where Ms. Dee set up her private station. It was large enough for her oversized station, her closet full of hair care products, and 5 extra chairs for her clients to sit in as they waited their turn. She enjoyed having the ability to close herself off from the rest of the shop to pray, meditate, or just to have some quiet time alone. She would also close her door when someone would come to her, in need of prayer or advice. There was a huge window in the front of her space, so she didn't miss anything when she closed her door.

Ms. Dee is one of those "saved, sanctified, and Holy Ghost filled" women. She was always giving the women who came to her advice, sound Biblical scriptures to back up what she was saying, and sometimes she would just fuss at the young women who admired her so much. She is 56 years old, but doesn't look a day over 40.

Ms. Dee looks good for her age. Her shoulder length black hair only has a hint of gray. Her high cheek bones, her smooth dark skin without blemishes or wrinkles kept us asking

2

about her beauty secrets. To which, she would always respond, "The Lord sustains me in my youth".

She is a woman of great faith. I have never seen this type of faith in God before, other than in my own mother. Ms. Dee had her first child at the age of 40. She believed God, and after much prayer and faith, she gave birth to her oldest daughter, Ki Anna. We all call her Kiki. Three years later, she gave birth to her son, Damien Jr. She had these two children after she had been told for years, by her personal physician, that she would *never* have any children. She always teases and says she should have named her children Miracle and Faith.

This neighborhood is where Ms. Dee was born and raised. She takes personal pride in the fact that she knows so many of the people who live in the neighborhood. She especially makes an effort to know the women and men who come into her shop. She believes that the closer she is to a person, the more she knows that person in the spiritual sense. Many times, she has helped people by speaking a word of encouragement when that person was suffering silently from some emotional wound. The person would not have to say anything about the thing that caused the suffering; Ms. Dee could *see* it on the person's face.

Ms. Dee is a woman we all respect, inspite of her daughter! Kiki works at the salon, mostly after school and on the weekends, answering the phones, washing towels, and keeping the place neat and clean. We all love and adore Kiki, but she has one problem—she knows everybody's business! When you think she is not listening, think again!

There have been times when Kiki has walked up to me while I was having one of my soul searching, need-some-good-advise conversations with Ms. Dee. She would listen attentively, with the intentions of grasping all of the information that she could, only to embellish the truth as she shared my problems with other people in the shop. Sometimes, especially when the matter was very private, I would just stop talking to Ms. Dee and tell Kiki to get her nose out of my business.

Ms. Dee started her Saturdays at 6:00 in the morning. She had this unwritten rule that whoever came in first on Saturdays had to help her open up. My friends and I were always the first ones on Ms. Dee's schedule for Saturday morning. We alternated who would come in first.

I remember the first time I came to see Ms. Dee. Marilyn had spoken with Ms. Dee and I was allowed to come in on that Saturday morning in Marilyn's place. Marilyn was scheduled for 6:30 and she warned me to be on time. I dared not to be late, so taking her warning seriously; I arrived at the shop at 6:15. I saw there was a truck in the parking lot and there were lights on in the shop. I made my way to the door and pressed the buzzer.

The door clicked and I entered in. Cautiously, I made my way past the barber area, past the dryer room, and into the salon portion of the shop, looking for any signs of life. I found Ms. Dee, in her booth, kneeling down in prayer at one of the chairs. I just stood there, too afraid to move. I didn't want to disturb the moment.

The moments seemed to drag, but I was not bold enough to make a sound in order to make my presence known. Ms. Dee had to have known that I was there, because she buzzed me and let me in the door.

"Good morning, young lady," the man's voice behind me caught me off guard. I jumped and quickly turned towards the voice and held my hands up in a defensive style.

"Whoa! Hold on now!" the man said. "I just wanted to say 'good morning' to you!" I let my hands down and tried to smile away my embarrassment. Obviously, this man was no threat.

"My name is Damien Hall. I Dee's husband," he said as he walked towards me with his hand held out to greet me properly.

"Hi. I'm Angela West," I said, shyly putting my small hand into his very large one.

"It's good to meet you, Ms. Angela," he roughly shook my hand and flashed a beautiful smile at me. "Be patient," he said, nodding his head in his wife's direction. "She'll be through in a few minutes, I'm sure. We've been here since 5:00. She's been praying and I've been fixing the washer in the back room. C'mon in the break room, I'll get you a cup of coffee."

I silently followed him to the break room not knowing what to expect. I am kind of shy that way. When I first meet people, I am very quiet around them. I begged Marilyn to come with me, but she insisted that I would be alright and she insisted that she was not going to get up early on a Saturday if she did not have to. Marilyn advised me that Ms. Dee would put me to work and as far as Ms. Dee was concerned, I would not be treated as a stranger. As a matter of fact, she would treat me like she has known me all of her life and I am one of the "children" she raised.

Mr. Hall directed me to the break room where he poured me a cup of coffee. It wasn't long afterwards that Ms. Dee joined us. She walked into the break room with this great smile on her face and her arms open wide.

"So you must be Angela! Come here and give me a hug!" Without hesitation, she walked right up to me and put both of her arms around me, giving me a great big bear hug. Momentarily, I felt as if I had just walked into my grandmother's house, for Sunday dinner and she'd grabbed me for one of those squeeze you real tight, swing back and forth, "look at my baby", grab your checks, and kiss you on the forehead greetings. I tried not to let my discomfort show.

"Let me look at you," Ms. Dee said, as she eased her death grip on me and leaned back so that she could look me over from my feet to my head.

I wasn't dressed in any fashionable manner. I just had on a pair of jeans, a pink tee shirt, pink sneakers, with a pink belt and baseball cap to accent my outfit. I have never really been the girly type and I've always found myself more

5

comfortable in a pair of jeans and whatever top I felt like wearing to complete my look and my mood.

"Now aren't you the cutest thing! Skinny, but cute!" Ms. Dee expressed, as she completed her examination of me.

"Cute?" I asked myself. "I have never really thought of myself as being cute. Skinny? Absolutely! But, never cute! I grew up with three older brothers! They teased me so much about how I looked that I never could see myself beyond their descriptions of me." I continued to analyze.

"Well, come on Angela, let's take a look at that hair of yours," Ms. Dee encouraged as she removed my cap from my head. I felt "naked" without my cap! My hair was a mess and was in desperate need of a perm.

Ms. Dee started running her hands over my head and through my hair, studying the ends and checking my roots. "You have beautiful hair!" She finally said. "Come on over here and let's get started!"

I followed Ms. Dee in the direction that she was walking. We were going over towards the shampoo stations. Then, without a word, Ms. Dee darted into the supply area. I patiently waited for her to return.

"Angela! Come on in here!" She shouted.

Slowly, I entered the supply area, apprehensive and somewhat confused. I peeped around the corner and observed Ms. Dee Standing in front of a large closet with shelves full of towels and supplies.

Ms. Dee grabbed an arm full of towels and handed them to me. "Here, grab these and start putting them in the drawers at the shampoo bowls," she instructed without even looking back at me.

Now, I was really confused! But, obediently, I grabbed the towels from her arms and left the supply room. I found Mr. Hall standing near the entrance to the supply room, still sipping on his coffee.

"I gather by that surprised look on your face, you thought when my wife said, 'Let's get started,' you thought she was meaning your hair! I guess Marilyn didn't tell you that the first customer of the day has to help my wife set up! Well, go ahead," Mr. Hall pointed towards the shampoo bowls, using the hand which held his coffee cup, "Get started!" Mr. Hall's shoulders shook as he laughed at me and my failure to fully understand my responsibilities as the first customer of the day.

I managed to feel my way through the shop, as I followed Ms. Dee's instructions for preparing the shop for the day. I cleaned toilets, wiped off counters, put toilet paper on the holders in the bathrooms, put out paper towels, mopped up the floor in the shampoo area, dusted, emptied trash cans, and lastly, refilled the snack machines and prepped two additional coffee filters for fresh coffee later in the day. All the while I was working; Ms. Dee turned on some Christian music then sat at her station and began looking over her appointment book.

As a shy person, I was unsure as to how I was going to respond to this salon-slavery. My immediate respect for Ms. Dee would not allow me to refuse any order that she gave, even though I had not cleaned out a toilet (because my mother had always done it), nor had I ever taken out any trash (because my dad made my brothers do it). Somehow, I felt that if I disobeyed her, God would be very angry me with me.

Nevertheless, I learned the routine, I grew to love Ms. Dee, and I learned to enjoy doing those small things for her, because she has shown me over the years how much she loves me.

Almost every Saturday since my first appointment at Ms. Dee's, I would meet my friends at Deirdre's Beauty Shop & Barber Salon. I was very glad that Marilyn introduced me to Ms. Dee when I let her know I was searching for a new beautician. I didn't know at the time, but Ms. Dee is more than just a beautician, she is a minister.

Marilyn has been a client of Ms. Dee's since the time she was getting her hair pressed. Ms. Dee has cared for my hair since the time I moved to Austin to attend college, up until now. My hair has always been past my shoulders and pretty thick. I have been very appreciative of the fact that someone else did it for me.

Not only that, but I have appreciated the way Ms. Dee could sense even when I was going through something, most of the time. I am a very private person, so I have always tried to keep my problems secret. I have always been one who would try to solve my problems on my own. Some times, however, we all need a little help with our weaknesses and we should not be ashamed or afraid to seek a little assistance.

Chapter 2

MY FRIENDS

♥

*I*t was another Saturday morning and it was six a.m. again. Today, it was my turn again to be the first one in. Ms. Dee was already in the shop when I arrived. She was praying in her booth as usual. As I turned on the lights, the bright pastel colors of the décor seemed to come alive. I started opening the blinds, putting out towels, filling the snack and soda machine in the breakroom, starting a pot of coffee, and checking to make sure the restrooms were clean. When I finished my preliminary duties, I found Ms. Dee checking and preparing her station. I waved my hand at her to let her know that I was there. She acknowledged me and continued doing her check. I continued prepping the shop as the smell of chemicals, coffee and blow dried hair slowly filled my nostrils as I moved around.

I could hear Christian music playing softly in the background. Ms. Dee believed in setting the atmosphere before she started working. After she turned on the music, she sat down in her chair to check her appointment book. It wouldn't be long before other people started to arrive.

While I was straightening up the counter at Ms. Dee's station, I saw the high school picture that I had given her. She liked receiving pictures of her clients. She had them posted all around her booth. There were pictures of weddings, proms and new babies. Some of her customers have been with Ms. Dee for so long, there were pictures of them from their early teens to the present.

Since I did not meet Ms. Dee until college, there were not any pictures of me when I was a little girl. The high school picture was one that I had left over as a senior. She insisted on a picture of me so I gave her that one. I paused my cleaning and picked up the picture. There I was, "Plain Jane". There was nothing special about the photo, although it was a senior picture. My hair was not fancy, there was not make up, there were no fancy clothes, I was just plain. I let out a sigh, dusted the photo and put it back in its place on Ms. Dee's stand.

I finished up the restrooms and went to the supply room where the washer and dryer were kept. As I was putting up the supplies, mop and bucket, I heard Ms. Dee calling.

"Angela Denise West"!

I don't know why she used my full name. She would do that whenever she was offering something parental to one of her younger customers and she would do that when she really wanted to get our attention. She said she called us by our full names just to remind us that she is our "elder", and as such, she deserved respect.

"Come on here so I can get started on your hair," Ms. Dee finished.

"Yes, ma'am, I'm coming!" I responded. I finished putting the supplies away, came out of the supply room and locked the door behind me. I smelled of bleach and pine cleaner! I didn't mind, though. I love and respect Ms. Dee. I think we all do. I quickly dried my hands on my clothes and rushed over to the shampoo bowl where Ms. Dee was waiting for me with shampoo in hand, a towel draped across her arm and running water. My hair was being shampooed when Marilyn walked in.

"Hey, Marilyn," I heard Ms. Dee say.

Without looking up, I echoed Ms. Dee's greeting to Marilyn and she responded. Marilyn went on into Ms. Dee's booth to wait her turn at the shampoo bowl.

Marilyn Boudreaux and I met in college. She and her family moved here after her father retired from the military to become a full time minister. She's kind of quiet, like I am. We were both brought up in church and considered ourselves to be Christians, although we both admit we were not perfect. Marilyn's father is the pastor of the church we both attend and until recently, he'd always kept tight reigns on Marilyn.

Marilyn has a beautiful voice and she considers that her greatest quality. I've heard her sing at many different places for many different occasions. She even sang the National Anthem at our college graduation. She also sings and plays the piano regularly at church, of course. There have been times when we all have traveled with Marilyn to different churches, to hear her sing on church programs. Although she has a great voice, she does not flaunt her gift.

She has always been concerned about her weight. She is not big in the sloppy sense. She's just a little over weight. Even at that, she always dresses nicely, not elaborate or extravagant, but very nice and neat. She keeps her makeup simple and Ms. Dee always has her long, beautiful hair done up in a fancy whirl of twist, candy curls and pin curls.

I also think she has the straighest, whitest smile I have ever seen! Teeth are a big thing to me, since I had to endure the pain and longsuffering of braces, my last years in high school. To me, Marilyn's million dollar smile is her greatest asset. Her vocal ability is just the icing on the cake.

Ms. Dee finished shampooing my hair and wrapped it in a towel. She called for Marilyn to come to the bowl and I went to wait in Ms. Dee's booth. As I was sitting there reading a magazine, Patrice came in, cheerful as usual.

"Hey, Patrice," I said casually, barely looking up from my magazine.

"Hey, Angela," she returned with a bubbly rhythm to her words. I stood up and we hugged as usual and then sat back down in my chair.

Patrice wasn't coming to get her hair done. She keeps her naturally curly hair either twisted up, braided, wrapped in some type of head covering or just naturally loose. This time, she had it braided with the braids twisted up on top of her head.

Patrice is one of those free spirited people. She does her own thing and doesn't let other people influence her. Her style changes daily. One day she would be dressed up like someone out of the 60's, the next day she would have on a dashiki, and then the following day, she would be dressed up like she was going to some futuristic Star Trek convention. She has no problem wearing mixed up colors, shades and patterns. At first glance, you would wonder what in the world did she have on, then after you stared at her for a while, you would begin to see and appreciate the freedom of expression she had when it came to the clothes she had on.

Patrice didn't wear make up. She didn't need to because her complexion is flawless. Her eyebrows are naturally arched and her features did not need to be improved upon. All she would wear is a little hint of eyeliner and mascara and some times, something light colored on her lips.

Patrice is always bubbly and cheerful. Rarely have I seen her angry or upset. The only thing, or should I say the only person, that seems to get her really upset is Derrick Freeman, her live-in boyfriend. Patrice seems to always end up with the wrong guys, but Derrick is the worse one yet.

Patrice was hired by Ms. Dee to run the boutique. She opened Ms. Dee's supply cabinet and grabbed the keys. She

12

still had a little time before she needed to open her shop, so she sat down to talk.

I have always enjoyed talking with Patrice. When she shared some of her problems with me, it made me realize that my problems were not that big compared to what she was going through. I admire that fact that although she was not raised by her mother, she has survived.

She calls her grandmother, "mother" and rarely talks about her mother. There are so many secrets in Patrice's life. Although we talk often, she hesitates to divulge any of her deep dark secrets. Whenever those secrets bother her, she will call me, even if it is in the middle of the night.

We have been friends for a long time. Of the three of my friends, I depend on Patrice the most. When I need someone to travel with me out of town, I call Patrice. When I need someone to be my "back-up" when I am facing a difficult situation, I call Patrice. She has this way of being there for me, without interfering with criticism or unwanted advice. When she is awakened in the middle of the night, because of her haunting past, she calls me. We have a strong mutually sharing relationship.

We continued in our casual conversation, waiting for the events of the day to come to past.

Chapter 3

REMO

♥

*M*arilyn and Ms. Dee came into the booth and Marilyn joined our conversation. Ms. Dee motioned for me to sit in the style chair, while she went about her station, gathering up supplies to prepare my hair.

We'd been talking about men in general, when the conversation changed directions.

"So, Angela, when are you going to settle down with somebody?" Patrice asked.

"When the right man comes along," I responded.

"What about Remo?" Ms. Dee asked. Remo came by every Friday, and paid Ms. Dee $100 for my hair. He didn't need to do that for me, but he did.

"What about him?" I asked.

"He cares a lot about you," Patrice said in his support.

"Well, you can have him," I told her, trying to maintain my composure.

"Girl, you know I'm already with somebody! All that money Remo spends on you! I sure wish he would spend some of it on me," Patrice said with a great big smile on her face.

"Have you slept with him yet?" Marilyn asked.

"No, and I don't plan to either," I said, feeling heat from the blood that was rising up in my face.

"Girl, you know ain't no black man gonna spend that much money on you and not expect something in return. Know what I mean?" Patrice reasoned, as she turned towards Marilyn, trying to get a positive response.

"Well, if that's the case, Remo can stop spending money on me today, right now, because I'm not going to sleep with him," I said, pointing my finger into the palm of my other hand, as if my actions could better portray my feelings. "Besides," I continued, "I never asked him to spend his money on me in the first place." I was trying to justify myself.

"I'll bet you ain't never told him to stop either!" Patrice confronted.

I sat back into the chair in a huff and folded my arms across my chest, trying to ignore the comments that were being made about Remo. They just didn't know him the way I do.

Even though we all laughed, Patrice's words hit me hard. I knew she was telling the truth. I didn't tell Remo to stop spending his money on me, paying my utilities, buying me clothes, jewelry, flowers for every occasion, or whatever he just wanted to do for me.

Whatever I needed or he thought I needed, Remo would get it for me. Why I would not tell him that his money was not needed is something I often asked myself. I had a good job. I often asked myself if I was allowing him to do the things he does because I was holding on to the security that his finances brought. Did I really need him to do for me what he does? I don't know. I wrestled with those thoughts too many times.

15

I met Reginald Morgan Douglas right here at Ms. Dee's one Saturday, about three years ago. I was getting my hair done and he was coming to get a hair cut. When he saw me sitting in Ms. Dee's chair, he came over to me and introduced himself as "Remo". Without my asking, he provided me with his real name and explained how people came to know him as Remo.

There were numerous times he would come to the shop, looking for me, with a dozen roses in his hand. This was even before I'd given him my phone number or anything. Although I really enjoyed his attention, there was just something about him that didn't sit well with me. His persistence and his gifts finally won me over, to an extent, and I went out with him. Since then, I have been trying to "let him go".

He works full time, at some industrial location and he has his own Disc Jockey business which he and his friends operate on the weekends. At first, his fans (so he called them) started calling him Reggie Mo'D. Later, his stage name shortened to Reggie Mo and lastly, it ended up as Remo. All of his *friends* and *fans* call him Remo. He gave me permission to do the same.

In spite of the fact that he had a good job working at the industrial location, he continued with his mobile DJ business that he and his friends started in high school. He started out with just a simple stereo system and an old truck to transport it in. After both his parents were killed in a car wreck, he inherited his parent's house and a huge trust fund. He used his trust fund to buy bigger and better equipment, a bigger truck and a trailer to haul all of the equipment around in.

Remo's truck reminded me of an intimidating freight train. It was one of those large oversized trucks. It has a double cab, with four full sized doors. With hydraulics and oversized tires, his truck stood higher than a normal sized truck. He had the truck customized with solid rims, a chrome grill on the front, 5 search lights on the top, and two chrome pipes were welded in such a way that Remo could step up on them and into his truck.

He finished his mechanical make over with fiber glass pipes. On top of that, he had it painted "midnight black" and then he had the windows tinted darker than the law would allow. The paint on his truck had this sort of iridescent look. Sometimes you would look at the truck and it would appear to be just black. Other times, when the sun hit it just right, it would look midnight blue. In the back window, in white letters were the words GANGSTER and REMO. GANGSTER was in the shape of an arch and REMO was situated within the arch.

The fiber glass pipes made the muffler roar when he drove down the street. Remo said he wanted people to hear him and know that it was him coming down the street. The black color of the truck glistened in the sun, and filled you with fear at night. The blue lights he had fixed underneath the truck gave it an eerie sort of sinister look. It was almost demonic.

In the bed of the truck, there was a chrome storage box that contained the speakers for his much too loud stereo system. The thumping bass from his music, coupled with the rumble from the pipes, really made Remo's truck fearsome. So many people have said how they hate the way they feel when they feel the vibrations, hear the noise and then look up in their rear view mirrors to see Remo's truck behind them.

I just hated the truck because when I felt it and heard it, I knew Remo was coming. I shuddered as my ears filled with the imaginary sound of Remo's truck coming down the street.

According to Remo, he and his two "partners" would profit anywhere from three thousand to five thousand dollars each, per weekend. He called it "tax free money". They would go to different cities in this area or hire themselves out for private parties or clubs. They would set up at the fair grounds, at different community centers and sometimes at a local park. The day before they were planning their gig, they would pass out flyers, letting everyone know where the "party" was going to be. People would show up, they would charge $5 to $10 a head, sell soft drinks and chips and the party would be on. They had enough equipment to set up for three parties simultaneously.

I appreciated the fact that they did not sell alcohol. Remo said it was because there was too much political paperwork involved in a liquor license and owning a building and he hated the thought of alcohol since it was a drunk driver that killed his parents. He was proud of the fact that his mobile operation provided a place even for young people to come and have a good time. Operating the way they did, they cut their overhead tremendously, ending up with a very profitable, cash only generating business.

Remo has his good points and his bad points. He seemed genuinely concerned for young people, but he did not know how to show his emotions well. He blamed that on the fact that his father physically abused his mother, but at the same time, he believed that his father loved his mother dearly. I don't know why he has such a hard time expressing himself. I just know there is something about him that makes him the wrong one for me.

Suddenly, my thoughts were interrupted by the loud talking that was taking place in Ms. Dee's booth. After turning my attention back to the conversation, I realized my friends were still talking about me and Remo.

"Yeah, Angela is going to keep her virginity forever!" Patrice screamed, as Marilyn and the other ladies joined her with their squeals of agreement.

"There's nothing wrong with that!" Ms. Dee defended me. "I was a virgin when I married my husband. That's the problem with you young girls these days. You think if you sleep with a man, or sleep with the man and allow yourself to become pregnant, then that will help you keep the man and marry the man. Well, if you've got to sleep with him to keep him, he's not worth keeping." All of the ladies grew silent as Ms. Dee continued. "By the time somebody comes along and he wants to marry you, you're already used, abused and loaded down with somebody else's children. A man would rather own a new car, than a used car, any day. Get what I'm talking about?"

Everyone was nervously silent. We all knew that Ms. Dee was telling the truth. I have seen too many girls give their bodies to guys who would just use them and toss them out. The truth is the *good* guys don't want to marry the *bad* girls. They want to marry girls they are not afraid to take home and introduce to their mothers. I think that is the major reason why I refuse to sleep with Remo. I know he is not the one I want to marry.

"And for your information," I broke the silence, "I won't be a virgin forever. I'm just waiting for the perfect man!"

Ms. Dee nodded her head, "Wait on him, baby," she said to me while spraying setting lotion onto my hair.

The other women laughed, trying to forget the impact Ms. Dee's words had on them. Neither of the ladies present could say they were virgins when they married, none of them except Ms. Dee, of course. They laughed mostly at me, teasing me about being an *old* virgin. Ms. Dee just stared at them, shaking her head as she combed the setting lotion through my hair.

Chapter 4

THE LOVE OF MY LIFE

♥

*P*atrice stood up to leave. It was time for her to open the boutique. Ms. Dee started rolling my hair. I hated this part. It seems to take forever, even though she was using large rollers. Oh well, it was another opportunity to allow my thoughts to drift.

As I began to mentally tune out everybody else's chatter, I started thinking about the first time I'd met the love of my life.

I was in college. It was shortly after I had broken up with Michael. He had been spreading rumors, telling all of his football buddies we'd slept together. He knew this was a lie! I was so angry! I felt violated, used and disrespected. I confronted him about the rumors and angrily ended our relationship when he admitted he made up the story of our encounter because he didn't "want to look like a punk in front of my boys", he said.

That night, I prayed to God, asking Him to allow me to meet the one I was to marry. I described to God what I wanted this perfect man to be like. I wanted him to be tall and handsome, soft sopken, gentle, loving, one who would never yell or curse at me, one who would love me unconditionally, and "oh yeah, a Christian", I remember adding to my prayer, "And God, if it's not too much to ask, let him have a beard". I think a man can be so handsome with a beard.

Then I added, "Oh, and Father, let this be a sign to me, when I first meet him, he will open the door for me". This was important to me. Men these days have gotten away from chivalry. They have gotten away from being polite. They have gotten away from being gentlemen. "That's what I want, God, a gentle man," I closed out my prayer.

A few months later, Patrice, Marilyn and I were selected to represent the young adult group of our church at a state convention. We traveled by bus, with the adult representatives, to Dallas for the convention.

When we arrived, we quickly discovered that the young adult representatives were not required to attend that particular conference. One of the adults instructed us to go to an empty room in the building, until they broke for lunch. We were disappointed to discover that we were the only young adults there, with nothing to do, nowhere to go, until.....

In walked this tall, extremely handsome, young man! All three of us stared at him as he walked towards us. I had stopped breathing. My eyes were fixed on his. I stared him up and down.

What caught my attention first was that beautifully perfect smile! It was topped with and surrounded by a light mustache and goatee. I could see there was potential for a full beard when he matured a little. His brown eyes were deeply set and so captivating!

I let out a small breath, inhaled again, and continued to allow my eyes to take in this perfect replica of my most imaginative fantasy.

21

He was tall, broad shouldered and his muscles were chisled to perfection. He was not overly muscular, just very well toned. His chest narrowed nicely into his waist, where his body regained momentum to fill out his buttocks and his thighs. His smoothly toned complexion was about the color of a vanilla waffer.

I gasped. I felt a drop of saliva forming on the bottom lip of my still open and now dry mouth.

"Hello, ladies," he spoke, not trying to be flirtatious or anything; just plain, "hello, ladies".

Patrice and Marilyn immediately began openly flirting with him. Marilyn started rubbing her hand on his chest while Patrice grabbed his arm and put it around her shoulder. They both held onto him, coaxing him to sit on a large desk that was near the door where he entered the room.

Through their flirtatious interrogation, we discovered he was from Fort Worth. He came to the conference as a favor to his mother. She just wanted him to ride with her. His name is Kenneth Ke-Mon (yes, with a hyphen) Williams, he plays basketball, he's 6'5", single, doesn't drink or smoke, do drugs and…

"I'm 17 and a high school senior. I'll be 18 on my next birthday this coming June!" he said proudly.

"Seventeen!" Marilyn shouted, quickly taking her hands off of his chest.

"A senior in high school!" Patrice echoed as she let go of his arm.

"Oh well," Patrice continued as she and Marilyn proceeded to walk away. "It was good while it lasted". They left him sitting there, on the desk, alone.

All the while they were flirting with Kenneth I sat quietly just taking in the view. He was wearing a pale yellow polo type shirt. It was unbuttoned. I could see the smallest hint of chest hairs peeking out of the shirt's opening. His black jeans were cut perfectly, accenting his lower body. He had his shirt tucked in and his jeans were belted – not like you see these guys who go around with their pants below their buttocks. No, this guy was different. He respected himself. You could tell by the way he was dressed.

Patrice and Marilyn left the room, saying they were going to see about lunch. I walked over to him, excited for the opportunity to be alone with him for a few moments.

"Hi," I said shyly. "Please forgive my friends. They are always embarassing me! (He smelled so good) I hope they didn't get too nosey".

"Oh, they were all right. I'm glad they left, though. I really wanted to talk to you".

My heart skipped a beat.

We engaged in casual conversation, talking about school, college, our dreams, what we wanted in a "special someone", and other bits and pieces of meaningless verbiage. It seemed like we talked for an hour, when suddenly, our conversation just stopped. I looked up and found myself staring into Kenneth's eyes, and he was staring back at me, with that overwhelming, breathtaking smile.

"Can I hold you?" his voice finally broke the brief silence.

"He said, 'Can I hold you, not hug you, but *hold* you,'" I thought to myself, trying to hold back a childish grin. I was trying my best not to rush into anything that I would later regret, so, "What if I said 'no'?", I asked.

"Then I would just pretend," Kenneth responded. At the same time, he closed his eyes, reached up and out with both his arms and grabbed the empty air, bringing his arms in close to his body. He wrapped his arms around his himself in a hugging fashion, swaying back and forth and caressing his shoulder with his hand. "This feels so good," he said, with his eyes still closed.

After taking a deep breath and exhaling, he dropped his arms to his side and opened his eyes.

I wished I was in his arms! "Hold me," I said, half out loud and half in a dream like state, before I even realized it!

23

Without saying a word and before I could resist again, he took hold of my hand and gently pulled me to him. As he did, he placed both my hands around his neck. I was almost forced to tiptoe because he is so much taller than I am. The smell of his cologne filled my nostrils as he embraced me. His face was caressing mine in such a way that I could feel his breath on my neck. The goose bumps quickly rose up on my arms, my back, then over every part of my body. I wanted that moment to last for ever!

But, as with all good things, this too came to an end. Kenneth kissed me right there at the base of my neck, where my neck and shoulders come together. I felt myself go weak in the knees. "Don't stop!" I shouted to myself.

Suddenly, my two no-sense-of-romance friends burst into the room, laughing and clowning around, saying they'd found a small soul-food restaurant within walking distance of the church. Kenneth and I separated, as if we were trying to convince them that we were not up to anything, as if they really cared.

"C'mon! Let's go get something to eat," Patrice shouted.

"Okay! I'm coming!" I responded back to her. I was so disappointed. I didn't really want to leave Kenneth. My mind was racing, thinking about the moment that just passed and the possibility of many more moments like that one, in my near future.

"Why don't you ladies go on ahead? I've got to check on my mother, and then I'll catch up with you," Kenneth stated.

We all agreed. My friends and I walked the two and a half blocks to the restaurant, chattering about Kenneth.

"He is so fine!" Patrice screamed.

"Yeah," Marilyn agreed, "but he's too young for me! I want a real man. He's still in high school".

"But, he's still so good looking!" Patrice tried to defend herself.

24

Marilyn, realizing I was kind of quiet, turned to me and asked, "Why are you so quiet? What are you thinking about"?

"Oh, nothing," I lied. I was thinking about kissing Kenneth's soft, full lips.

We walked into the restaurant, went through the serving line and payed for our own selections. We found a table near the center of the dining area. Quickly, almost without thinking, I sat in the chair that was facing the door. I wanted to see Kenneth when he walked in.

"Well," Marilyn started, "since you are the youngest out of all of us, you can have him. Go ahead and ask him for his number".

"What do you mean, since I am the youngest?" I asked, almost offended.

The truth is, I am the youngest of the four of us. It was March. I had just turned 19, and was about to finish my freshman year in college. Patrice was 19 and about to turn twenty. Her birthday is in July. She is also a freshman in college. She decided to take a year off after completing high school, before starting college. Marilyn turned 21 by the end of the year.

"What do you mean? I can have him! I don't need you to let me have somebody!" I retorted. I wasn't angry, but I did feel my confidence coming forth.

"As a matter of fact," I continued, "before I leave here today, I'm going to get his number, his address and--," I paused and snapped my fingers to add emphasis to my courage, "...a kiss!"

Right about then, my hands started shaking. I hid them under the table to keep my friends from seeing that my new found courage had been dipped in fear, sprinkled with shyness, yet with just a hint of desperate anticipation. I really wanted that kiss.

"We dare you!" Marilyn challenged.

"No, we bet you $20 and dare you!" Patrice increased the stakes.

"Okay," I agreed, nodding my head in false confidence, "if I don't get all three – the phone number, address, and the kiss, I'll give each of you twenty dollars apiece. But, when (I emphasized "*when*") I do, you two are going to give me twenty dollars apiece!"

We were finishing up our little wager as Kenneth walked in. He quickly went through the serving line and joined us at our table. Not wanting to embarrass myself by dropping food on my lap, I got up from the table to empty my tray. As I was returning to the table, the three of them were huddled together. I saw Kenneth nod in agreement with some devious plot as Patrice and Marilyn broke out in hearty laughter. I made a note to myself to keep my guard up. Those two were always making me the brunt of their jokes.

When I approached the table, they all became quiet and began busying themselves over their plates. Their actions made me uncomfortable. I searched each of their faces, trying to get a hint as to what they were planning.

They finished their meals. We cleared the table and walked back to the church. Patrice and Marilyn were engaged in light conversation with Kenneth, while my mind was working overtime trying to devise a plan to get this guy, who I just met, to kiss me. It wasn't that I was afraid of loosing the money. It was the principle of the thing. I would never be able to live it down if I was unable to make good on this dare. Besides, I *really* wanted to kiss him!

"C'mon brain! Think!" I was so nervous with anticipation and expectation.

We made our way back to the church and found the room we were originally in. Before we could get comfortable, one of the adult representatives came into the room and asked for a volunteer to go to all of the other classes and have all of the other adult representatives to reconviene in the main sanctuary.

Without thinking, I volunteered first, "I'll go!"

Kenneth quickly jumped to my side and said, "I'll go, too!"

Not being out done, and apparently not wanting to let Kenneth and me out of their sights, Marilyn and Patrice also volunteered, saying, "Why don't we all go!"

We went from room to room, notifying the adults that it was time for their particular sessions to end. I wanted the four of us to divide up into two groups to make the process move along faster. Kenneth agreed with me, but my two couldn't-catch-a hint-if-it-was-a-virus friends refused to leave us alone.

Finally, all of the classrooms were empty. We started back towards the main sanctuary. Kenneth and I were walking behind my friends, with Kenneth walking slightly behind me.

"This is my chance," I thought, as I slipped into an empty room. I hoped against hope that Kenneth would come in behind me.

"What are you doing in here?" I heard his mild voice ask.

I turned towards him, "I thought there were some people in here," I lied, "Guess not," I paused, trying to quickly come up with a way to ask for a kiss without seeming too forward. "It's kind of warm in here," I said, trying to make light conversation.

"Yes, it is," he answered, as he walked towards me. I felt my heart beat increase. I thought he could hear it pounding against my rib cage. There he was standing right in front of me, not touching, just standing. I was looking up into his eyes. The moment seemed like an eternity.

"Can I...," I felt myself whisper. But, before I could finish my question and ask him for a kiss, he said in a most manly voice, "Yes," as he gently grabbed me by shoulders and pulled my body to his. As he leaned towards me, I closed my eyes and opened my mouth slightly to receive his kiss---Perfect! Every fiber of my being tingled!

Before I could document the moment in the diary of my mind, a crashing sound at the door awakened me from my fantasy.

"What are you doing?" screamed Marilyn as she and Patrice burst through the door. Kenneth broke out into a laughter that came from deep with in his throat. His eyes sparkled as he leaned his head back, still laughing.

"What is going on?" I asked nervously. I just knew they were laughing at me and once again, I was the victim of one of my friend's jokes.

"We told him you were going to ask him for a kiss. And you," Marilyn emphasized as she turned towards Kenneth and pointing her finger in his chest, "you were supposed to tell her 'NO'!"

"But, I wanted to kiss her!" Kenneth said, still laughing, emphasizing the word "wanted". We all laughed and called off the bet.

We went back to our room of assignment where we chatted and made light conversation until it was time to leave. As much as I wanted to be alone with Kenneth, I was glad my friends were there to help me keep the conversation going. Finally, it was time for us to load up on our bus. Marilyn and Patrice were kind enough to leave me in the room alone with Kenneth, so we could say our goodbyes.

After additional conversation and promises to keep in touch, Kenneth kissed me again. I held my breath again, not wanting the moment to end. As we turned to walk out of the room to make our way to my bus, Kenneth jumped ahead of me saying, "Let me get that for you". He opened the door and ushered me through. I could feel warmth rushing to my cheeks as I blushed in the presence of his chivalry. My heart skipped a beat when I remembered my prayer for a sign. I asked myself, "Is this the one?"

He walked me all the way to the bus. My friends had already entered the bus and found their seats. Not wanting to be embarrassed by the many eyes staring at me from the bus, I tiptoed and kissed Kenneth on his cheek before he could lean towards me for one last kiss. I entered the bus, reluctantly, wondering if I would ever see this man again. Only time would tell.

On the bus ride home, I reached into my pocket and pulled out the crumpled piece of paper that Kenneth had written his phone number and address on. I stared at it, reliving each kiss. He signed the note,

> *"I'll cherish our moments together,*
> *Until we met again.*
> *--Kenneth Ke-Mon Williams*

"Okay, Angela," Ms. Dee's voice brought me back to the beauty salon and back to the present. "I'm finished. Get on up and go to the dryer room."

From that first kiss to the present time was about seven years. During that time, Kenneth, the love of my life would be coming in and out of my life.

"God! Why can't he just come in and *stay* in?" I asked in my thoughts.

I love him—at least I think I love him. My chest hurts whenever I think about him. It's like I can't breath! Is this love? I can't seem to get him out of my mind. No one can compare to him. It hurts! I mean, my heart literally hurts when I think about him and realize how far apart we are. But, at the same time, it feels *so* good!

Chapter 5

GHETTO-FABULOUS!

Ms. Dee finished rolling my hair and I stood up to go to the dryer room. I looked up and saw Ya'Shika coming in, followed by her three children; Lexus, Mercedes, and Toya.

Ya'Shika is one of those big, Ghetto-Fabulous girls who thinks she is so fine! At that time, she was twenty-three years old with those three children. Of course, they all had different fathers.

"Whoop-BAM! Whoop-BAM!"

That was the sound her body seemed to make as she walked through the shop, moving her hips from side to side just a little too much! She walked in wearing a much too tight, too little denim skirt, a halter top, and big earrings. Ya'Shika's big belly was straining, trying to remain within the confines of her tight skirt. There was a dent in her belly where her navel was supposed to be. It was peeking out over the waist band of her skirt. And, of course, her make up was always too much! Even though it looked as if it had been applied by a professional,

Ya'Shika always wore too much eye shadow, too much eye brow liner, too much bright fuchsia lip stick, just too much of everything on her face and not enough of anything on her body!

She often bragged about how she named her children after the cars she was making out in when she became pregnant. The oldest girl, A'Lexus, looked like a little genius with her thick glasses and protruding teeth. From what I have heard, though, she is pretty smart. Mercedes, her second child, was actually a cute little 6 year-old. Her curly brown hair, light brown complexion and hazel eyes helped to substantiate Ya'Shika's claim that her father is a white man.

Toya is the youngest. Ya'Shika said that "Toya" is short for "Toyota". I am so glad that even Ya'Shika had enough sense not to name that girl Toyota. Toya is a cute little 5 year-old. In fact, she is so cute it is hard to believe that Ya'Shika is her mother. She never would let us know who her father is, as if it was some kind of well guarded secret.

As Ya'Shika entered the shop and walked past the men in the barber area, I could hear one of the customers shouting, "What in the hell is that smell?"

I could imagine he covered his mouth and nose to keep the smell from getting into his mouth.

As always, Kiki pulled out a can of air freshener, and just began spraying vigorously into the air. She was spraying so much that the guys in the barber area started coughing. At that point, Kiki followed Ya'Shika back towards Ms. Dee's booth, still spraying.

"Okay, Kiki," Ms. Dee ordered, "That's enough".

"Momma, that girl stinks! I told her don't be coming up in here smelling like that! She needs to take a bath," Kiki replied, ignoring the fact that she might be embarassing Ya'Shika or hurting her feelings.

"Mind your own business, Kiki," Ya'Shika said while throwing up her extremely long fingernailed hand in Kiki's face, and rolling her neck.

31

The truth is, Ya'Shika did stink! Everyone in and around Ms. Dee's booth had put their hands over their noses and mouths, except Ms. Dee of course. A few people left the area to get a breath of fresh air. I sat back down in a chair, resisting the temptation to cover my face, just to see what was going to happen next. I needed a good laugh.

"Ms. Dee," Ya'Shika started, "I need you to do my hair."

Ya'Shika's hair consisted of her short black hair, which was in desperate need of a perm, being gelled up into a past-the-buttocks, tangled, need-to-be-cut-off-and-buried, orange, brown and black colored *phony* tail extension. It looked like she was wearing a tiger's tail on her head.

"Do you have any money, Ya'Shika?" Ms. Dee asked. "This is not a social service organization, you know."

"Ms. Dee, I got $100 left on my Lone Star card," Ya'Shika said as she pulled her food stamp credit card out of the front pocket of her tight denim mini skirt. "You can use it to buy you some groceries. My hair is only gonna be $50, but you can use the whole hundred," she continued to bargain.

"Didn't your water get turned off? You were in here yesterday, trying to get $50 with your card so you could get your water turned back on," confronted Kiki. "You need to be trying to get your water bill payed instead of trying to get that nasty hair of yours fixed," Kiki said angrily as she tossed up Ya'Shika's pony tail to further stress her point.

"Kiki, you can kiss my…," Ya'Shika started to say.

"No, I can't," Kiki blurted in, "I ain't got all day". Kiki finished her statement, turned in a huff and went back up front to her desk.

Of course we all cracked up laughing. Not fazed in the least, by the remarks and the laughter, Ya'Shika went from bargaining to begging. "C'mon, Ms. Dee, please! I got a date tonight and I can't have my hair looking like this!" she cried.

"Ya'Shika, you need to be taking care of these kids with that money," Ms. Dee said, pointing at the three children. "Go get your babies something to eat and work on getting your water turned back on."

We could see that Ms. Dee was getting angry. This wasn't something she did very often, but when it came to kids and sorry mommas not taking care of them, Ms. Dee would get mad! She is a firm believer that children are a gift from God and when mothers don't take care of their children it is a disgrace to Him.

Another reason she would get angry is the fact that she had to pray so hard and wait so long, before she could get pregnant and have a child of her own.

"I told you, Ya'Shika, the last time I did your hair for free, that I was not going to do that again. And, I'm not taking your food stamps either!" Ms. Dee shouted, pointing a comb at Ya'Shika.

"Ms. Dee, please," Ya'Shika begged, still displaying the Lone Star card in her hand, "What do you have to loose?"

"My integrity"! Ms. Dee stood her ground, slamming the comb on her counter. "Now, get out!" Ms. Dee pointed towards the exit, "Don't come back in here until you have some money and all of your utilites are paid!" Ms. Dee commanded in a stern, serious voice.

Ms. Dee was serious about that. She would make Ya'Shika show her that all of her bills were paid before she would take money and do Ya'Shika's hair. Taking care of your children is that important to Ms. Dee.

I've even seen her help people. One of her clients came in one Saturday to cancel her appointment because she'd been layed off from her job and didn't have any money. The lady was visibly upset. Ms. Dee could sense that something else was wrong. The lady confessed she was in need of food for her family.

Immediately, Ms. Dee went through the shop and asked everyone in there for five dollars apeice. Ms. Dee is well respected. Every one gave, without even asking any questions. Several of them gave more than she asked.

Ya'Shika turned to leave, seeing she wasn't going to get anywhere with Ms. Dee. Her children followed her in silent obedience.

"Oh, well," I thought to myself, "Show's over. Guess I'll go to the dryer room."

I was walking a few steps behind Ya'Shika. Boy, that smell was awful! It was a cross between dead fish, sour milk and wet dog! I held my breath and took another step back. All the while I was behind her I couldn't take my eyes off those rolls of flesh bulging out from under her tank top. That top looked like it belonged to her daughter, Toya!

I looked down at her feet. Why did I do that? Because I was trying not to focus on that sweat that was building up between her thighs! All that fat rubbing together! And she had the nerve to be wearing that denim mini skirt!

Her feet were so ashy! A gallon of grease couldn't penetrate that ash! She had squeezed her big feet into a pair of open toed mules. It always amazed me how big women could wear those high heeled shoes without any problem.

Don't get me wrong, there's nothing wrong with being a *big* woman. I have seen many beautiful big women. Marilyn is one of them. The only problem I have with big women is when they go to the boutiques for small women and squeeze themselves into styles designed especially for small women. Not only did she wear clothes that were not for her, she stank! Ya'Shika was always a walking, twisting, flirting, shaking, stinking, fashion disaster.

Ya'Shika walked towards the barber's area as I turned towards the dryer room. I paused briefly. I looked up just in time to see Ya'Shika offer up her best flirtatious smile to the men. In the mirror that lined the wall in the barber's area, I could see her pink tongue peeking through that huge gap in her front teeth. The men just stared. I went into the dryer room.

Suddenly, I heard a bunch of groans and sounds of disgust coming from the barber area. I looked back out. Ya'Shika had "dropped" her Lone Star card on the floor!

With her behind facing the men, she was bent over, picking up the card! I didn't even want to think about what the fellows saw that made them enter into their vocal chorus of moans and groans!

One of the guys even ran from his seat with his hand over his mouth and nose, past the dryer room to the restroom, making gagging noises! Ys'Shika smiled again, and twisted her fanny as she walked out.

"She wasn't wearing any panties!" I heard one of the men wail.

I shuddered and walked on into the dryer room to take a seat under the dryer.

Chapter 6

MS. "BAM"

♥

*W*hen I stepped into the dryer room, I was somewhat disappointed to see that I was going to have to take the unlucky seat in the corner. All of the other dryers were taken. Before taking the unwanted seat, I heard the bell on the door ring. I looked up and saw Beverly Ann coming in. Beverly Ann hated her name. She's 29 years young and has such an ancient name. Her mother is mixed, being half white and half African-American. She named Beverly Ann after her mother, Beverly Ann's grandmother. She has disliked her name forever.

As a matter of fact, she used to say that the only reason she became an attorney was so she could change her name. She's been an attorney now for 6 years and her name is still Beverly Ann Marvell.

Since she didn't want us calling her Beverly Ann, or Bev, or Ann, we have resorted to call her BAM because of her initials. She wanted us to call her Marvell because it is short for marvelous, but we chose to call her Bam. She's gotten used to that name and it has become her trademark, so to speak.

I have admired her, ever since we became friends in college. "Bam" was 21, when I first met her. I was a new freshman and she was a senior. We became friends immediately. She said I was like the little sister she never had.

She has always been the aggressive one in our group. Bam sets her agenda, makes her plan and sticks to it. She was determined to finish college in less than four years, and she diligently pressed forward to reach her goal. She graduated in the December before the end of her fourth year. When she graduated from college I was inspired to press forward and do the same. The following January she began law school.

Not only have I admired her spirit and her intellect, she is a very beautiful black woman, to me. Bam is 5'11" tall, has smooth caramel colored skin, and a very well proportioned figure. Her hazel eyes (natural, of course), her thin lips and high cheek bones serve to remind her of her mixed ethnic background. I have always said that she would have been a beautiful model.

Whenever I see her, she is dressed "to the 9's" or better (meaning on a scale of 1 to 10, she is always at a 9 or higher). Even on Saturday mornings, she would come to the beauty salon with her make up on perfectly, her clothes, shoes, purse, and nails would all have the same color scheme. Her short cropped hair always looked as if she's just stepped out of the salon. Every so often, she would change her hair color, "to match her mood". Most recently, her naturally brown hair had been invaded with golden brown streaks. Even at that, Bam's style just couldn't be duplicated.

Bam was offered an attorney's position, even before she graduated, with the firm where she completed her internship. She is one of the best criminal defense and family law attorneys in this area. She preferred family and criminal law over civil and business, saying, "guilty people will always pay to stay out of jail, and as long as people are getting married, there will always be people who have children and get a divorce".

She has made a pretty good start in the legal arena. Her success has provided her with the finances she has always dreamed of. She owns a 3 bedroom, two and ½ bath condo, with a two car garage. She has a black BMW with BAM-01 on the license plate and a cream colored Lexus with BAM-02 on the license plate. When I asked her why she has two cars, she simply replied, "I have a two car garage, so I put two cars in it".

Although she has made her mark in her career of choice, she has failed miserably in the area of love and marriage. She has been married three times in the last six years, with all three marriages ending in a nasty divorce. She always says that the divorces were nasty because the men she married came into the marriage with nothing but they were always trying to leave with something. She's an attorney, so she refused to let that happen.

Bam openly admits that the first three times she married it was all based on the flesh. She chose her men based on how good the man looked and how well he performed in bed. She didn't concern herself with their financial or emotional stability, saying she made enough money and had enough confidence for her husband and herself.

Her second husband was the most pathetic, in my opinion. He was an older gentleman. After they married, Bam learned that the only job he'd ever had was a paper route, which he left shortly after the marriage vows were spoken.

Bam's first husband was the most brutal. We all hated him. Bam said he changed shortly after they were married. He first wanted her to quit her job and be a housewife. When she told him that she would not, his attitude changed and the abuse started. On the last occasion, he beat her so badly that her jaw was dislocated. She stayed in the hospital for several days due to her jaw and internal injuries.

No one had to convince her to divorce him. After the divorce was final, Bam was determined not to let any man beat up on her like that again. So, she found out from the local police department that the female officers taught self defense classes specifically for women. She took as many of the classes as she could. She continues to work out and practices her self defense tactics on a regular basis. That, no doubt, is the reason she looks so physically fit and toned.

Her last marriage was so brief, none of us even know who he is and Bam is not telling. There are no pictures of him in her house, she has never "slipped" and said his name, and she only refers to him as "nightmare number three".

With three marriages and 6 years down the drain, Bam promised herself that the next time she married it would be for love and she's going to make sure that the man she marries has more, and makes more money than she does.

Every time Bam walked into the shop, all of the men in the barber area would stop what they were doing, in mid-motion, and watch her walk from the front door to the back where Ms. Dee's station is. Sometimes, one of the men would get brave and speak, then the rest would follow suit. This was one of those mornings. I could hear the male chorus in the barber shop.

"Good morning, Ms. Bam!"

"How're you doing, Ms. Bam."

"You look real nice today, Ms. Bam."

"Have a good day, Ms. Bam". She just stared at them. She rarely responded.

The men always called her "*Ms*. Bam". They didn't do this for just *any* woman. Bam just has that kind of beauty and grace that captures everyone's attention. When she enters the room, the women would be green with envy and the men would drool.

This particular morning, Bam walked in wearing a light blue, sleeveless tee-shirt, a pair of light blue, slip-on shoes, and a white mini shirt. She had the right kind of legs for a mini skirt. They were long, smooth, and muscular. All twenty of her nails were done with ice blue polish, with silver and white accents. She completed her look with silver jewelry.

Bam walked back to Ms. Dee's station without saying a word. Although she walked with an air of arrogance, her confidence seemed to be the more powerful trait of her personality. She wasn't a snob, as so many people think; she's just confident. Her walk let everyone know that she knew she was in control of her life. I'm just glad to have her as my friend.

My dryer finished and I returned to Ms. Dee's booth so that she could put the finishing touches on my hair. When I arrived at the booth, I found Bam sitting in a chair, patiently waiting for her turn. This gave us the opportunity to talk. I was a little intimidated by Bam, even though she is my friend. I found myself constantly comparing myself to her. She seemed so much more mature, so much older than I.

She's a promising attorney. I'm just a school teacher, working at the prison, trying to teach grown men enough elementary education so that they can obtain their GED's. She has experienced so much in life, and I am still a virgin. She looks so great, all the time! Me, I'm just a plain Jane kind of person. She has this beautiful golden brown skin, mine is a dull sort of crayon brown. She has her BMW and I have my Ice Blue Mustang.

She is more like a big sister to me, as opposed to a friend. I could always count on her to provide me with good stern advice when I needed it. She has also come to my rescue a time or two. And, like a big sister, she is always easy to talk to.

When I look at her, I think to myself that I want to be like her when I "grow up". She's strong, confident and so independent. I grew up very sheltered. I never stayed out past midnight while I was living at home. I was the *good* child growing up. I didn't talk back to adults, always said "yes, ma'am", and "yes, sir". I have never cursed. As a matter of fact, I have not been allowed to use a lot of street slang or "ghetto language", as my mother called it. I don't drink, I've never thought about smoking, and...I'm still a virgin! What a life! What a boring life!

Bam and I continued making small talk and Ms. Dee soon finished my hair.

Chapter 7

GUESS WHO'S DRIVING YOUR CAR

I was on my way out of the salon when my cell phone rang.

"Hello."

"Oh, Lord, it's Patrice" I thought, "What kind of crisis is she in now?" I listened.

"Can you come take me home? I've been waiting for Derrick for over an hour and he hasn't picked me up yet," she said.

"Are you ready to leave now?"

"Yeah, I just need to finish up some sales tickets."

"Well, I'll walk on over to the shop and wait for you. It's kind of warm out here."

I walked the short distance between the salon and RAG Apparel. I enjoyed looking at all of the things Ms. Dee had in her shop. I especially enjoyed looking at those fluffy, fluffy dresses, dreaming of the day that I would have a little girl to wear them. Patrice, as the manager, had the opportunity to search through different wholesalers to find these unique dresses that would be in the shop. Mothers could also find matching socks, panties and bows to go with the dresses.

There were some Christian tee-shirts in the store, too. I browsed through them while Patrice was finishing her paperwork. They were so interesting. One of them had on it, a drawing of Christ on the cross, with a huge drop of blood falling towards a drawing of the earth. The caption read: "Universal Blood Donor." This shirt sent chills through my body as I thought about the sacrifice Jesus made. I decided I wanted that shirt.

The next shirt I selected to buy was one that had a huge lock and key on the front. The caption read: "Prayer is the Key, but FAITH will make you get up off your knees and work!" I guessed that meant that after you get through praying about something, you need to do the work that follows.

I laid the shirts on the counter and told Patrice I wanted to purchase them. Patrice emerged from the small office in the rear and completed the sale for me. She finished the day's sales and prepared the deposit bags for Ms. Dee's husband to pick up later. She locked up, set the alarm and we were finally ready to leave. Derrick was still nowhere to be seen.

We got in my car and we prepared to pull out of the parking lot into traffic. Patrice started going on and on about Derrick. Derrick Freeman is Patrice's live in boyfriend. Derrick has been in and out of trouble for as long as we all can remember. Bam and I believed he was doing drugs. Marilyn doesn't care, and Patrice is blinded from the truth.

Derrick was always late picking Patrice up. He doesn't have a job and he doesn't have a car of his own. He is forever dropping Patrice off in her own car and picking her up late. Shortly after we entered traffic, I heard Patrice's voice.

"Is that my…," Patrice's voice trailed off and she sat up in her seat and focused her attention on a red, four door, Mitsubishi Gallant, coming down the street.

"That's my car!" Patrice shouted and pointed at the car by pressing her finger at the closed window, as we passed a car that looked very much like hers.

Patrice has a very nice car. It is a red, 1999 model, with a sunroof and stereo. It's not new, but it's hers and she is very proud of the fact that she bought and paid for it herself. Bam offered to help if she needed to, but fortunately for Patrice, she was able to get into the car without any assistance from anyone. She even managed to have her tags personalized with her nickname, "Peaches". Okay, on her tags it's spelled "PEA-CHZ", but they were personalized all the same.

Patrice had turned her body halfway around, she screamed and said again, "THAT'S MY CAR! And some little heifer is driving it! Turn around! Turn around!"

I managed to pull into the next parking lot, make a quick turn around and got into the flow of traffic, following that red car. It was easy to spot. The traffic wasn't too heavy so it was pretty easy to catch up. When we got right behind the car, we could clearly see that it was Patrice's car, but that sure was not Derrick driving!

We pulled up next to the car, Patrice rolled down her window. Now she was really mad. The person driving her car was none other than Ya'Shika Mo'Nay Johnson! We could only imagine how she managed to get Patrice's car from Derrick!

"Ya'Shika! Pull over!" Patrice was yelling, hanging out the window, and shaking her fist at Ya'Shika. Ya'Shika stuck her tongue out at Patrice and kept driving.

Patrice pulled her body back into my car.

"Can you believe this heifer? What is she doing with her big fat behind in my car?" she asked me, knowing I didn't have the answer.

44

"I couldn't tell you, Patrice," I said, trying to sound sympathetic. I have been trying to tell her for the longest that she needed to get rid of Derrick. He is just no good.

Patrice leaned her body out of the car again, and shouted even louder at Ya'Shika, "PULL MY CAR OVER RIGHT NOW, YOU FAT WITCH!"

Ya'Shika must have sensed the seriousness in Patrice's voice because she pulled over into the next parking lot. I managed to get over and pull into the parking lot right behind her.

As soon as I stopped, Patrice jumped out and ran over to Ya'Shika in her car. Ya'Shika was in the process of pulling her big body out of Patrice's car by the time she caught up with her.

"Get out! Get out! Get your fat, stank, greasy behind out of my car!" Patrice shouted as she emphasized her disgust with her actions. She was jumping around, rolling her neck, weaving her head about and pointing at Ya'Shika.

"Take yo' car, you old thang!" Ya'Shika shouted back as she finally pulled her body out of the car.

"I want my hundred dollars back!" Ya'Shika shouted as she held out on hand and put the other one on her hip.

"What are you talking about?" Patrice argued with her.

While all of this was going on, I was just watching! I pulled an apple out of a snack bag in my car, leaned against my hood, and just watched. I wasn't about to mess up my hair that I just had done at Ms. Dee's! This was a perfect comedy show and I had a front row seat!

"I gave Derrick my Lone Star card and he said I could borrow his car for an hour. My time ain't up yet so I want my hundred dollars back!" Ya'Shika yelled, with her hand still sticking out, wanting Patrice to fill it.

"As you can see, you pre-school drop out, this is NOT Derrick's car! I'm not giving you a thing!" Patrice said, pointing at the license plate. "Now give me my keys before I snatch what's left of that nasty pony tail out of your head!"

"Yo' keys is in yo' car!"

Patrice stuck her head into her car to verify that the keys were in the ignition.

"Ooo, you funky witch! My car stinks!" Patrice threw her hands in the air in disgust.

"Angela, can you give me a ride?" Ya'Shika asked me, now standing with her big arms folded on top of her breast. Yes, they were on TOP of her breast!

I almost choked on my apple. "Girl, you better run over to that bus stop and catch that bus! Here, I'll even give you dollar for bus fare, but you are not getting your funky tail in my car." I told her. I reached into my pocket, pulled out a dollar, and waved it at her.

Ya'Shika cracked one of her I-don't-care-smiles as she walked towards me and took the dollar out of my hands. I turned my head to the side and held my breath as she got closer to me. She turned to walk towards the bus stop which was right on the edge of the parking lot.

I could see Patrice still examining her car, shielding her nose and mouth to keep the smell out. She had opened all the car doors to let the air circulate through, hoping to rid the car of the smell.

"Oh, my god! No she didn't!" screamed Patrice. I had to go over to see what was causing her so much grief.

"Look at what that nasty girl left in my car!" she screamed as she pointed down at the back seat floor board. I followed her pointing finger. There on the back floorboard was a used condom!

"And my car stinks like hell!" Patrice was whining now. "Ooo, I'm gonna kill Derrick! But first, I'm gonna kill…" Now she was really mad! She started muttering to herself, and frantically searching in the trunk of her car for something. I was still eating on my apple, when she emerged from her car with a huge knife!

"This oughtta take care of her!" Patrice said, holding the knife up in front of her face, examining the sharpness of the blade. She started a quick paced walk towards Ya'Shika who

46

was still at the bus stop. I decided I'd better step in or else something was going to happen that we would all regret. I dropped what was left of my apple and started running after Patrice.

"Patrice! What are you doing?" I screamed as I was running.

"I'm fixing to cut her!"

"You can't do that!"

"Why not?" Patrice was still going towards Ya'Shika.

"Girl, you would go to jail!" I said as I caught up with her.

"Yeah, but I would feel a whole lot better!"

"C'mon, give me the knife!" I begged

"Just let me cut her one time," Patrice still had her eyes focused on Ya'Shika. The bus was approaching. I grabbed Patrice's arm, trying to slow her down. She kept moving forward, getting within arm's reach of Ya'Shika.

"Ya'Shika, get your big ol' fat self on that bus!" I screamed, trying to save two lives.

The bus door opened, Ya'Shika put her foot on the step to enter just as Patrice was close enough to put her hand on Ya'Shika. Just as Ya'Shika pulled her body up onto the bus, Patrice grabbed that below-the-butt phony tail and gave it a hard yank. Ya'Shika's head snapped back. As the bus door closed, Ya'Shika turned towards the doorway, staring at Patrice with one hand on her head and her mouth wide open in horror. Patrice stood there with the tiger's tail in her hand, holding it up in victory. We laughed, Patrice put the hair in a nearby trashcan and we walked back to her car.

"Why don't we take your car to get it cleaned? I'll even pay for it." I suggested.

"Okay," Patrice agreed, "but first let me find out where Derrick is. Can I use your phone?"

I gave her my cell phone. Derrick had her phone. We all knew that Derrick's credit is so bad that he couldn't even get a cell phone in his momma's name!

"Hello?...Hello?...Derrick!...Derrick!"   Patrice screamed increasingly into the phone. She angrily clicked the button on my phone to disconnect.

"What happened?" I asked.

"Derrick! He makes me so sick! He answered the phone and said, 'He ain't here', and hung back up! Why do I put up with him?"

"Come on. Let's get your car cleaned."

I followed Patrice to an auto detailing service. The working supervisor explained it would take several hours, due to the number of cars ahead of Patrice's. So, we left the car, with a promise to be called as soon as it was ready.

I took Patrice home to her apartment and decided to go up and wait with her until her car was finished. The apartment consisted of the huge open room with a living area, small dining area and kitchen on the side. There was one bathroom and one bedroom.

I sat on the sofa and took a look around. It had been awhile since the last time I was at Patrice's place. It was moderately decorated, not fancy at all. The color scheme was burgundy and navy. She had several plants throughout the living area.

Then, something really caught my attention. There was a new frame on her wall that I didn't remember seeing. I got up to take a look at it. I couldn't believe it! There on the wall, in Patrice's living room, framed and hanging proudly, were Derrick's parole discharge papers! I was standing there, laughing, when Patrice came back in the living area.

"What is it?" Patrice asked.

"I can't believe you have Derrick's parole papers hanging in your living room!"

"Derrick did that"

"But in your living room, Patrice?"

"Yeah, it is kind of stupid isn't it," she said as she was now standing next to me, looking at the proudly framed document.

Without saying another word, Patrice took the papers from the wall; frame and all, walked over to the trashcan and dumped the whole thing. I clapped my hands in agreement. Patrice was still standing over the trashcan, looking at the parole papers. She reached into the trash and pulled it back out.

"What are you doing?" I asked, as I hurried back over to her, "you put that right back in there, right now!" I was afraid she was having second thoughts.

"Girl, all I'm fixing to do is take these papers out of here and throw them back in the trash. I'm keeping this frame, though. It's a cute frame, girl," she said, holding the frame up so that I could see it again.

We laughed. I helped her take the papers out of the frame and put the papers back in with the other trash.

About that time, I received a phone call on my cell phone from the auto detail service shop. Patrice's car was ready.

When we arrived to pick up Patrice's car, we found there was a plastic bag containing some items, sitting on the front passenger seat. One of the attendants saw the looks on our faces and saw us examining the contents of the bag, so he came over to explain. He let us know that when they are cleaning the interior of the vehicles they service, they place all of the items from the floor board and from underneath the seats in a bag, unless the item is obvious trash such as used food containers, or other things that had been used. He was trying to be sarcastic, but we failed to see the humor in his statements.

Patrice had been going through the bag while the attendant was explaining. She screamed as she pulled a pair of purple panties from the bag.

"Oh, hell naw! These are not my panties and they are too little for Ya'Shika! I'm gonna kill Derrick!" she screamed, clutching the panties in her fist and shaking it in the air. For the first time, she acknowledged the fact that Derrick was cheating on her. Everything that we, her friends, have been telling her for the longest time was consolidated into that one pair of purple panties.

I let her rant and rave for a moment. I wanted her to really get angry so that she would hold on to that emotion when she confronted Derrick about what she'd found in her car. She didn't show too much anger about the fact that Ya'Shika was driving her car; she only got a little angry when she found the condom, thinking that Ya'Shika was the one responsible. But, now, she was holding reality in her hands and she reached the point where she was furious. I was not going to take that moment from her, so I just let her vent.

After she let off some steam, I was able to convince her to throw those nasty panties in the trash. She made a promise to herself to confront Derrick the very next time she saw him. Whether she did or not, I don't know. Rumor has it that she did confront Derrick and he told her that the panties and condom belonged to his cousin. All I can say is, if she did confront him, she didn't tell anybody about it.

Chapter 8

THAT'S MY BABY'S DADDY

I made it through my week at work without any problems. I was so glad it was Saturday morning again. Bam came in first this time, so by the time I arrived, she was already gone. Marilyn was already under the dryer.

Ms. Dee shampooed and wrapped my hair and I went into the dryer room. The ladies in the dryer room were already in the process of choosing their baby's daddy by the time I took my seat. One lady was even looking at Fat Boy. He is one of the barbers and is just big and fat.

"He has a sweet personality," the lady said.
"With that body, he needs more than personality!" one lady cackled.

"I'll bet he would take care of his children, though," another one added.

"But could you imagine waking up next to that every morning for the rest of your life?" one of them laughed.

"I'll take him," said the one who was larger than the rest.

"Who is that other tall and thin barber?" an older lady asked.

"That's her cousin," Marilyn said, pointing at me. "Be careful what you say about him"

"I was just going to say how fine he is!"

Prince, my cousin, is really cute. He is tall, about 5'11, and musclular, but thin. He eats all the time but never seems to gain any weight. Prince always wears jeans, tennis shoes, and tee shirts. He wears his jeans loose but starched. He says the loose jeans make him look "bigger" than he really is. He keeps his long, natural hair braided back, with black beads on the ends. The fact that he lacks facial hair makes it difficult for people to guess his age. He's two years older than I am, making him about 28 at the time.

His name is actually Everson Lamar Prince II. I call him Prince because he doesn't like to be called Everson or Lamar. And besides, Prince is kind of a cute name. Other people think his first name is Prince. Neither he nor I have taken the time to let people know that Prince is actually his last name.

Prince lives with me in my house. The split floor plan is perfect. He has his side and I have mine. There is a bathroom on his side that he uses, and I use the one in the master bedroom where I sleep. Prince is also very handy with tools and carpentry. I allowed him to remodel the two bedrooms on his side, to make one huge open room. He built an archway between the two rooms. He uses one side for his sleeping area and the other side, he has made into a sitting room, where he watches his TV, keeps his computer, and his stereo. With the kitchen, dining room and living room being between our two sides, it's easy for us to have our privacy.

"Oowie! That man is shaped like an 'X'! All them muscles! I could just...mmmm!" one of the women purred. I looked over my magazine and saw that she was getting real excited about someone who'd just come in.

It wasn't long before I realized that the person coming in was Cedric Mitchell. Ced, as I call him sometimes, is a member of the police force. The shop is in his area so he stops by regularly to "check on things". Ms. Dee appreciates him coming by, so Prince agreed to give him a discount rate on his hair cuts.

Cedric is built like a brick! No matter what he had on, you could plainly see his muscles bulging! Cedric takes great pride in his body and has even participated in some semi-professional body building competitions.

The lady was right in describing his body as the letter "X". Cedric's broad shoulders, thick, tight, rock hard chest, six pack abs, narrowed at his waist. His big thighs and calves complete the bottom half of the letter "X". The great thing about Cedric is, he's single and has no kids! I think he is waiting for the perfect woman.

Marilyn's cell phone rang.

"Hello?" I took my attention away from my magazine again, to eaves drop on her conversation.

"You what? Who is this?...You...what?...Oh, no you didn't!" I could see Marilyn getting upset with whoever it was on the phone.

"Who was that?" I asked as I lifted the dryer hood up to make sure I heard her response.

"That was one of Darius' baby's mommas!"

"What did she want?" I dropped my magazine to my lap after I realized Marilyn was becoming upset.

"That cow was calling me, asking me where her child support check is! Can you believe that"!

"Oh, girl! No she didn't!" I said in agreement.

"I paid Darius' child support last month because he lost his job again. But I would just have to really be out of my mind if I paid it again this month!"

The phone rang again.

"Hello?" Marilyn's voice was shaking a little and I was eaves dropping, trying not to be obvious. "Besides, she's my friend and I am justified!" I argued with my conscience while still listening to Marilyn's private conversation.

"NO! I don't know where your momma's child support check is!" Marilyn shouted into the phone and then disconnected.

"Who was that?" I asked again.

"That, was one of her kids, calling and asking me if I know where his momma's child support check is! I am sick and tired of Darius' kids and their mommas!"

Marilyn's voice was wavering. I could tell she was really upset.

Darius Devon Boudreaux was Marilyn's husband. Prior to that, he was the biggest "mack daddy" on campus! Yeah, he is cute to the bone, with his yellow complexion and curly hair (not naturally curly, he keeps a wave kit on it). He was not athletic, not muscular, just really, really cute! He was always dressed nice, with slacks and buttoned down shirts.

His biggest problem is that he treats women like dogs! While we were all in college, he didn't respect any of the girls he dated. He used them, slept with them, got five of them pregnant and then tossed them out with the trash. Unfortunately, Marilyn was one of his "victims". Altogether, he has six children, and five baby's mommas.

We all have been wondering why Marilyn married Darius. We think it was because she became pregnant and her father, who is my pastor, was not going to let Darius just sleep with his daughter and toss her out. Although Marilyn lost the baby during the pregnancy, due to a miscarriage, she has stayed married to Darius. I don't think Marilyn's father would let her get a divorce.

Through the years, Darius has worked off and on, not keeping any one job for over a year. If the truth be told, he's been off more than he's been on. Marilyn has taken care of him financially forever. She pays the note on his Nissan Maxima, while she continues to drive the Ford Taurus her father gave her when she married Darius. Even when he does not have a job, he dresses like he is someone off the cover of a male model magazine, in clothes that have been purchased, of course, by Marilyn.

Darius is the epitome of a sorry man. He would sit at home all day, in his robe, playing at the computer, claiming to be working on some big business deal. When Marilyn would come home from work, he would ask her what she was going to cook for dinner!

I looked over at Marilyn. She was fidgeting with her phone, trying to turn it off, I guessed. Finally, she turned her face to the side and folded her arms across her chest. She was still breathing hard, still angry with the woman and her child calling about the child support.

I shook my head, thinking about how disgusted I would be, if I was in her same situation. I can't blame it all on Darius, though. If it was me, I would have divorced him the day after I lost the baby. I had to remind myself that Darius did not force Marilyn to sleep with him and she could have stood up to her father when she became pregnant.

Seeing Marilyn in her situation, and even seeing so many other women who became *accidentally* pregnant before marriage has been more than enough motivation for me to stay a virgin until I am ready for all of the potential "side affects" that premarital sexual activity can bring.

As Ms. Dee said, too many young ladies these days give their bodies away too quickly, settling for what they can get instead of believing God for what He wants them to have. I've seen more than enough young women become pregnant trying to get and keep some man. Me? I can wait!

The other ladies tried to turn their attention back to the men in the barber area. I returned my attention to my magazine.

Chapter 9

ONE SINGLE ROSE

♥

The ladies in the dryer room continued their oogling and their comments. I let them have their fun, since I was not in a position to see anything. I poured my attention into a magazine and tried to concentrate on the article I was reading, "How to Love Your Spouse".

The title caught my attention, but I was almost disappointed when the writer, Dr. K. Johnson, started talking about the article being about "*loving* your spouse", and not "*making* love to your spouse".

As I kept reading, the article became very interesting. Soon, I was so into the article, that I barely heard the oo's and aah's the other ladies were making as someone who was described by one of the women being as "delicious" entered the barber shop.

I looked up at them, over my magazine, made a face, and went back to my reading. From where I was sitting, I couldn't see who came in the door. I was in the unlucky seat, the one that sits in the corner where you can't get a clear view of who was coming or going.

I tried to ignore them as they continued their conversation.

"He's so fine!"

"He is so tall!"

"And handsome! I love that beard."

"Girl, look at that toned body…"

"Who is he anyway?"

"I've never seen him before.

"He's so fine!"

"Girl, for sho', that's gonna be my baby's daddy!"

"He can be your baby's daddy, I just want him to be my man!"

They cackled and screamed with laughter. I just ignored them.

"He's walking around like he's looking for somebody."

"Is that a rose in his hand?"

"What is he doing wearing that suit in the barber shop?"

"I hope he's looking for me!"

"Here I am, baby!"

"Shut up, girl! He's coming in here!"

"Ooowie! He really is tall!"

I kept trying to ignore them. Besides, not only was I in the unlucky seat, but I didn't have on my contacts, and I'd left my glasses at Ms. Dee's station. I wouldn't be able to see him unless he walked right up in fromt of me and….

I felt the sudden silence in the dryer room that interrupted my thoughts. I looked up to see what was going on. There he was, standing right in front of me!

"Kenneth," I said, barely above a whisper. His bright smile made my heart flutter. He was standing there, with one single lavender rose in his hand. He looked so good!

I lifted up the hood of the dryer, my mouth was open. I was trying to say something, anything! My mind was moving so fast with all of the words I wanted to say.

Then my thoughts shifted. I was so embarrassed! There I was, sitting there with all of those rollers in my hair; no make up, and I was dressed in raggedy clothes! At first, I just knew it was not going to be a good day.

While my thoughts were racing, Kenneth leaned over and gave me a long kiss. At the same time, he laid the rose and a note on my lap. He kissed me a second time.

I opened my eyes after the second kiss and he was gone. I looked around to make sure I wasn't dreaming. All of the women in the dryer room were staring at me. I *knew* at that moment I was not dreaming.

"What?" I asked sarcastically and stared back at them. I wanted my attitude to say to them, "This happens to me all the time! Doesn't it happen to you, too? Don't be jealous!"

I focused my attention on the note while all of the other women stared, still in disbelief. The note card smelled like the cologne he was wearing. My hands were shaking as I opened the note. I read these words:

A unique rose
A unique woman
A unique relationship

His note went on to tell me that he was going to be in San Antonio through that Monday. He wanted me to come join him at the Plaza Hotel. He gave me directions and instructions to ask for a message at the counter. He wanted me to come, but would understand if I couldn't. After I read it, I held the note in my hands, close to my chest, took a deep breath, closed my eyes and tried to envision the romance that was about to take place.

"What's it say?" one of the ladies asked.

"What?" I asked.

"What did he say in his note," Marilyn asked.

"That's none of your business!" I smiled at all of them. I just leaned back, replaced my dryer hood, and inhaled the aroma from the rose that Kenneth had just given to me. I closed my eyes and let my mind drift.

I thought about the many rendezvous that Kenneth and I shared over the years. My favorite is the time when I met him in Arlington to go to the amusement park. I remember that it was so hot! It was about 116 degrees that summer. Kenneth and I walked around the park, trying to stay in the shade. There were so many people collapsing in the heat! I wasn't worried about being overcome by the heat because at that time, I only weighed 105 pounds, soaking wet and I never, ever sweat!

Kenneth was the perfect gentleman that day. We walked hand in hand, he helped me in and out of the many rides, he held me tightly when I was afraid (or pretended to be) and he never let me out of his sight! He'd even won one of those large teddy bears for me at a basketball shooting booth. All of his attention was on me and his goal was "to make you happy; this is your day," he said to me.

It wasn't until mid-afternoon that I realized how much he cared about me, even in our distant relationship. There we were, standing in the sun, watching one of the side shows. Suddenly, I began to see spots, I couldn't hear, my head was spinning and everything seemed to be moving in slow motion. I knew I needed to sit down.

As I turned slowly and looked up at Kenneth, I could see a look of horror spread across his face. In my mind, I was telling him that I needed to sit down in the shade, but my body was slowly falling towards the ground! Before I completely passed out, Kenneth swooped me up into his arms, with the greatest ease, and took me to a shady spot. He immediately asked someone to get some water for me.

Fortunately for us, there was a first aid wagon close by. The driver saw me falling and hurried over to assist me. Kenneth insisted, against my complaints, that I be taken to the infirmary until I recovered. I released my strong will when he said he was going with me because he didn't want to let me out of his sight. He wanted to be sure that I was alright, and "besides, I wouldn't have any fun without you!" he said.

Chapter 10

WHEN LOVE HURTS

♥

I was still sitting there with my eyes closed, day dreaming and thinking about my many encounters with Kenneth, when a commotion broke out in the barber's area. I could hear a young girl screaming.

"Somebody help! Come quick! Somebody's beating up on Patrice!" she screamed.

By the time she finished her statement, several other ladies and I had already abandoned our dryers and went into the barber area where we could hear more. As soon as the little girl said "Patrice", Prince dropped his clippers and took off running towards the boutique where Patrice was working. Cedric followed behind him. Of course I had to go see what was going on.

By the time I got to the boutique, Prince had Derrick by the back of his shirt, pulling him off of Patrice. He jerked Derrick around so that he could speak to him face-to-face. He was yelling at Derrick, threatening to kill him if he hurt Patrice again. Derrick was stumbling backwards, trying to get away from Prince, but he managed to keep a firm grip on Derrick's shirt. It was obvious that Derrick was high or drunk or both.

Derrick took a weak swing at Prince, trying to get him to loosen his grip. That swing just angered him more! Prince quickly laid three firm blows on Derrick's chin and face. Blood trickled from his mouth and nose. Derrick was barely conscious.

Prince dragged him to the front door where Cedric was watching calmly, and I was standing next to him, with my mouth and eyes wide open in amazement. Prince regularly defended me, but I'd never seen him this physically aggressive with anyone else.

As Prince came closer to the door with Derrick, Cedric stepped to the side and I went over to Patrice. She was still sitting on the floor, next to the counter, crying exhaustively. I could clearly see the swelling over her eye and the blood on her lip. Both wounds were obviously the result of Derrick hitting her.

I looked back over my shoulder to glare at Derrick as I kneeled down next to Patrice. I opened my mouth to say something sarcastic to Derrick, but before I could, Prince tossed him out of the shop, onto the side walk.

"Don't come around here anymore!" Prince shouted.

Cedric just looked on. Sometimes he just did that. If two people were involved in a "minor" dispute, he would act as sort of a referee and watch. If he thought Prince was really going to hurt Derrick, he would have intervened. He knew, from past experience, that Patrice would not be willing to file charges against Derrick. I think that's why he didn't stop Prince from doing what he did.

As far as Ced and I were concerned, Derrick deserved everything that he got from Prince. Cedric stepped outside the shop and warned Derrick if he came around again, he would arrest him for Criminal Trespassing. Derrick left on foot, stumbling off to some unknown place.

I went to the little restroom in the rear of the shop and wet some paper towels for Patrice's face. By the time I returned to her, Ms. Dee had arrived and was trying to get Patrice to calm down. She was still crying when I handed her the paper towels. She put them on her face and began trying to explain to Ms. Dee what happened.

"Derrick came in here, asking me for some money. When I told him I didn't have any, he reached across the counter, and tried to get into the cash register. When I grabbed his hand," she explained between her tears, "that's when he came behind the counter and hit me! Then he started shaking me and screaming at me, telling me to open the cash register! When I still wouldn't open it, he hit me again," she paused. "I'm so sorry, Ms. Dee."

"For what, baby? Everybody in here knows Derrick's got problems. We just want *you* to realize it," Ms. Dee reassured her. "I would rather you give him every dime in that drawer, as opposed to you risking your life for a few dollars. You are more valuable than that to me and to God!" Ms. Dee hugged Patrice and then helped her to her feet.

"But, I love him, Ms. Dee, and I believe he loves me too," Patrice confessed through her tears.

"Love is not supposed to hurt, Patrice," Ms. Dee firmly stated. "When love hurts, it is definitely not love. Love is gentle, kind, sacrificial, patient, caring, sharing, giving, protecting and so much more. What Derrick did to you today, is definitely not love!" Ms. Dee emphasized by shaking her head. "When are you going to realize that? You have to realize it for yourself. All the rest of us can do is pray for you." Ms. Dee gave Patrice a hug to let her know that her words were not meant to hurt, but to convince Patrice that she needed to let Derrick go.

Several others in the group of spectators came closer and gathered around Patrice, giving her hugs and words of encouragement. I felt tears swelling up in my eyes as I stood behind Patrice. I could feel the genuine concern that these strangers displayed. Marilyn and Bam came up to Patrice as the crowd left. We all gave her hugs and Bam started in again.

"Patrice, I have told you to get rid of that sorry, broke down, excuse of a man. You are too smart and too cute for such a *little* man as Derrick. And, I stress the word little." She held up her hand, with her thumb and pointer finger extended to give us a visual of the word "little".

We laughed at the thought. After we calmed Patrice down and dried her tears, we all helped Patrice straighten the shop back up. Ms. Dee telephoned and told Patrice to close the shop for the rest of the day and go home.

Patrice decided to go to her grandmother's house and promised not to go back to her apartment alone. The rest of us returned to the beauty shop so that Ms. Dee could finish our hair. This dramatic episode was over.

Chapter 11

SHATTERED DREAMS

I Returned to Ms. Dee's and finished drying my hair. All the while, I was dreaming about my appointment with Kenneth in San Antonio. My mind was racing with fantasies that only he could fulfill. With every thought, my heart rate seemed to pick up its pace.

Finally, my dryer clicked off. I went to Ms. Dee's booth where she was finishing the touches on Marilyn's hair. Marilyn and my friends knew about Kenneth. However, They did not know how much I still cared for him. Neither did they know the full extent of my wishful relationship with him. They just thought we were *good friends*, since I was supposed to be with Remo.

The truth is, I didn't tell them because I knew that they would talk. If they talked, Remo would eventually find out. If Remo found out that he is not the love of my life, I just didn't want to imagine what he would do to me. I didn't tell my best friends about my greatest dream, frankly because girls, sometimes, just talk too much.

Marilyn searched my face for answers as we stood up to change places. Ms. Dee had finished her hair and it was my turn to take the style chair. I maintained a secure smile on my face, praying that she could not read my mind. She would probably try to talk me out of going to San Antonio.

I'm so glad that she left the shop after Ms. Dee finished her hair. I didn't want her to be in my presence too long. She would eventually ask questions about Kenneth and his reasons for coming to the shop or take the well guarded note from my hand and my secret would be out.

As soon as Ms. Dee finished my hair, I stood up to leave, reaching into my pocket to withdraw a $50 bill to pay her with. Instinctively, I remembered that Remo probably already paid Ms. Dee with a $100, giving her a fifty dollar tip. I shoved my money back into my pocket after Ms. Dee confirmed my thoughts, justifying myself with the fact that I may be financially able to pay for my hair, but I cannot afford a $50 tip. I looked at the rose in my hand, gave Ms. Dee a hug and left the shop to prepare for my trip.

All the way home, I kept visualizing how the weekend would be. I imagined Kenneth filling the room with flowers, ordering fresh fruit and having soft music playing in the back ground. I even dared to envision him asking me to marry him. Now that, is a real fantasy.

I reached my house, ran inside and started packing as quickly as I could for my trip to San Antonio. Since I didn't know exactly what Kenneth had planned, I packed a variety of things. I chose a dressy black dress that Remo bought for me when I needed a fancy dress for a banquet. It still had tags on it. (I decided not to attend the banquet when Remo insisted on escorting me). I grabbed 2 short sets, 2 negligees, 2 pairs of jeans and tee-shirts, a pant suit, underwear, swim suit, several body sprays and gels, and the necessities of course.

I was in the process of closing my suit case when I felt that all too familiar feeling rise up in my chest.   "No, it can't be!" I said out loud to myself. I hid the suitcase in my closet and gently laid the rose and note on the top shelf in my closet. I held my breath as I ran to the front window and peeked out. As I did, the roar of Remo's truck filled the air, filled my ears, filled my house, and finally rumbled through my chest as he pulled his truck into my driveway, behind my car.

I jerked the front door open, filled with a brief bit of courage. As Remo walked towards my door, I tried to think of something strong to say to him. Why is he here? What did he want? I kept asking myself.

"What do you want?" I finally asked him.

"I just came to check on you. I heard what happened to Patrice at the shop," He replied. His voice always sounded harsh, even when he was trying to be protective. I didn't trust him.

"What do you mean, 'check on' me? I don't need you to check on me, Remo," I said, still blocking the door and not allowing him in.

"I don't want that punk, Derrick to come by here and do something to you," he said as he put his hand on the door, above my head, forcing the door open. He looked down at me as he stepped through the doorway in spite of my weak attempt to resist.

Remo sat on my sofa, put his feet up on my coffee table and turned on my TV with the remote. Okay, even though he'd bought all of those things, they were in my house. They belonged to me. If he insisted on owning them, he could take all of the items back to his house and watch the TV there. I was angry that he made himself so comfortable in my house.

"Remo, you can leave now. No one is coming to hurt me. Cedric was at the shop when Derrick attacked Patrice. He knows better than to come here and try to do something to me. Besides, if I get scared, I can go to Bam's house or Patrice's apartment," I said, trying to convince him to leave, so that I could leave.

"Well, you don't have to worry. I got it all worked out," Remo said with confidence. "I'm gonna leave my truck here tonight so if Derrick comes by here, he will think I'm here and keep going," he finished, as he reached into his shirt pocket, grabbed a tooth pick and put it in his teeth. Remo has never spent the night at my house so I couldn't understand why he thought he could fool Derrick into thinking he was here. No one would believe that I let Remo stay the night with me.

"No! I want you to leave!" I shouted without thinking. My heart went before my head and now my head might have to pay the price. Remo jumped up off the sofa and came to the other side of the coffee table where I was standing, with my hands on my hips, trying not to let my fear creep through.

"Who you think you...girl, I told you don't be playing with me! I promised to take care of you and that's what I'm gonna do!" He was standing right in front of my face with his finger pointing close to my nose. I took two steps back, trying to get out of his reach.

"Come here, let me show you something," he said, trying to calm himself down. He would get so angry so fast. I know that he has restraint, but one day, I imagine he will just explode and I would be the victim of his wrath.

"No, Remo. I don't want to go with you. I want you to leave," I resisted, in the calmest voice I could.

"I'll leave, but first I want to show you something."

"No, Remo!" My voice was a little raised due to the increased stress I was feeling as the situation progressed.

"I said I just want to show you something!" he said in a loud, almost yelling voice. He grabbed the upper part of my arm and pulled me towards the front door. I knew better than to resist, so I went with him to his truck, hoping he would ease his grip on my arm.

He unlocked the back door on the driver's side and reached for something behind the seat. I heard a click and the lower portion of the rear seat popped up. He reached inside the dark space and withdrew a locked metal box. After unlocking the box he said, "Look at all of this," he grabbed a hand full of bills, "it's for you," he paused. "Look, baby." He shoved the bills in my hands then grabbed a bank book from the box. He showed me his balance which read $150,275.54 (Yes, I stared at it long enough to read the entire amount). He shoved the bank book into my hand and pulled some savings bonds from the box. At a quick glance, I could see that the bonds totaled over $10,000. I was not impressed. I guess he could see the look on my face.

"See, baby, I can give you what ever you want!" he smiled, waiting for a positive response from me.

"Remo, I don't want…"

"Well, what do you want from me then?" He yelled, throwing his hands angrily in the air. "I can give you everything! Why are you so…"

His voice was interrupted by the honk of a horn. He looked over his shoulder to see one of his friends pulling up to my driveway. Without saying a word, he grabbed all of the money and the bank book from my hands and put them back into the metal box. He closed the box, closed the seat, locked up his truck….and left, leaving his truck to protect me, he says—to block me in is what I say.

I beat my fist into the air, pretending I was beating on Remo's chest. Then I turned and went inside my house, stomping as I did. I was angry. No, I was livid! How dare him! How dare Remo keep me from going to San Antonio! He was not my boyfriend, but he thought he was and acted as if he was. He was so possessive! He told everyone that I "belonged" to him.

I kept going over in my head trying to figure out what I did or said that made him believe that I wanted him. When I first met him, he'd walk into the salon and give me a dozen roses almost every Saturday. I was flattered and accepted, but, what he did not understand or realize is that there was more meaning, love and passion in the one rose given to me by Kenneth, than there was in all of the dozens of roses he has given me—all put together!

I went to my room, trying to come up with an alternative plan. I grabbed the note card from my closet and read the number to the Plaza Hotel where Kenneth would be staying. Without a second thought, I dialed the number. I would leave a message for Kenneth to come and get me. The phone rang two times and the voice of the receptionist filled my ear.

"Good afternoon, Plaza Hotel. How can I help you?" the voice asked.

"I…" my mind started thinking as I held the phone in my hand.

"Hello?" the voice asked a second time.

"I…" my mind visualized Remo returning to my house, just in time to see Kenneth either pull up or leave. I just knew that Kenneth would suffer greatly in Remo's hands, if Remo ever saw him at my house. As a matter of fact, any man would suffer greatly if Remo caught them at my house, no matter how innocent the situation. At that thought, I slammed the phone down without leaving a message.

"Ooo, he makes me so sick!" I yelled to the top of my lungs and aimlessly swung my arms around in the air.

I paced back and forth in my bedroom, trying desperately to come up with an alternate plan. I couldn't call Patrice; she had enough drama for the day. I really didn't want to call Marilyn or Bam because they would want to know why I wanted to go to San Antonio tonight. Catch a bus! No, I had no way to get there and no way to get from San Antonio's bus station after I'd arrived. The pacing, thinking, pacing and planning, lasted for over an hour, with no positive results. I felt defeated! My dreams of a most romantic weekend had been shattered!

Mentally exhausted, emotionally frustrated, and physically drained from the events of the entire day, I fell back onto my queen size bed, with both my hands extended over my head. With my eyes closed, I continued my mental quest to devise a workable solution to my problem.

Finally, somehow, after much planning and scheming, I found myself in San Antonio. The Plaza Hotel was easy to locate. I pulled my rental car into the parking lot and into a space near the front door. After removing my bags and my delicate lavender rose, I locked the door and made my way to the front counter.

Before Kenneth saw me at Ms. Dee's, I had not seen him for a while. I was so anxious to see him I could hardly stand the wait! My mind was filled with all types of fantasies. I told myself that I was a virgin today, but I might not be one tomorrow! That thought made me excited and nervous at the same time.

I felt so nervous as I walked up to the front desk and asked if there were any messages for me. As Kenneth promised, the clerk handed an envelope to me with my name on it. Inside the envelope, there was a room key and a note that read: "I'm glad you're here! Go on up and make yourself comfortable. I should be there about 8:00. I plan to take you to dinner. See you soon!"

The note had a hint of his cologne. I closed my eyes and brought the note closer to my face and inhaled deeply to fill my nostrils with an immediate vision of Kenneth.

Finding the room was simple. I walked in and discovered that our simple hotel room was actually a two bedroom suite! I sat my bags down near the door and began exploring the room. As I stepped past the small foyer, the suite opened up into a large room that served as the living area, a small table and chairs for dining, and a small kitchenette. There was a room on the left of the living area and another one to the right.

"Okay," I said out loud to myself, "Let's see which room is going to be for me."

I walked over to the room on the left. I immediately knew this was where Kenneth planned to sleep. The room contained two double beds. Kenneth's suit bag was already laid out on one of the beds. I imagined he removed one of his suits for the business meeting he was attending. His cologne and other personal items were neatly arranged on the dresser. His shoes were neatly lined up at the foot of one of the beds.

More anxiety filled me as I ran the short distance between the rooms to take a look at where I was sleeping. My room was filled with flowers! The aroma filled the air. There were rose petals sprinkled on the queen sized bed. As I was taking in the view and the aroma, I turned around the room slowly. There, on the dresser, was a crystal vase filled with lavender roses! I ran to them to examine them closer. I saw a note sitting next to the vase with my name on it. I opened it and read these words:

"You are the only one who could make this picture complete! Thank you! Kenneth".

Closing my eyes, I took in a deep breath as I held the note close to me. When I began to smell the fragrance from each rose, I realized there were only eleven. The dozen was incomplete. Then I remembered the single rose that Kenneth brought to me earlier. I rushed to the foyer where I'd left my bags and my rose. I hurried back to the vase and placed my lonely rose into the vase with the others, making the picture "complete".

Then, as I continued taking in the view of the room, I fixed my eyes on a white gift box that was also on the bed, in the midst the rose petals. I walked over to get a closer look. I saw the small card underneath the violet ribbon that had my name on it.

I could hardly contain myself as I eagerly ripped the box open. I pulled out the most beautiful dinner dress I had ever seen! The midnight blue color was dazzling! It was embellished with silver trimmings and tiny beads. It was designed to fit snuggly from the top and down towards my waist. From there it flowed freely from below the waist down to about an ankle length. I held my breath as I held it up to my body to get a preview of the fit. Perfect!

The clock on the nightstand indicated it was a few minutes after seven. I quickly got into a rush to prepare myself for whatever Kenneth had planned. I showered, put on my makeup and styled my hair. Lastly, I slipped into my silver colored dress sandals and put on the dress purchased by Kenneth. I held my breath as I pulled the dress up past my thighs, my hips and then my waist. I slipped the spaghetti straps over my shoulders and proceeded to zip the dress. Fortunately for me, the zipper was on the side.

I examined myself in the mirror and was pleased with what I saw. As I was putting on my silver earrings, I heard Kenneth entering through the front door.

"Niecy?" he called to me.

"Here I am," I responded, exiting the bedroom and anticipating his first glance at me.

Slowly, he turned towards my voice. A smile crept up on his face. I could see why he chose midnight blue as the color for my dress. He was standing there in a double breast, navy suit with the palest blue shirt and tie. I walked towards him, not taking my eyes off of his. I tried hard to keep from grinning too much.

"I'm so glad to see you," he said as he pulled me closer to him, finally embracing me with both his arms. This hug is one that I have waited for, for so long. I let out a slow breath as he tightened his arms around me. This just felt so *right*.

The rest of the evening was pretty much a blur. There was dinner and dancing, a walk along the river, and much conversation about business, and catching up on each other.

The evening ended well after midnight. We took a slow stroll through the hotel's lobby. On the elevator ride up to our room, Kenneth leaned over and gave me a long slow kiss. I was glad the elevator was empty. I did not want others to share in

74

our private moment. Only the mirrors that lined the walls of the elevator were able to capture the memories of our actions.

When we entered the room, Kenneth, of course, opened the door for me. After he shut the door behind himself, we both turned towards each other, both of us eager for another kiss. I felt passion rising up in me, as well as in Kenneth. He grabbed me closer to him, and continued kissing me.

I asked myself if I was ready. I believed I was. It was the right man and the right place. But, is this the right time? That was one of the things my mother taught me. Sex can be a great thing, providing three elements are in place: the right man, the right time and the right place. If either one of these elements was missing; the encounter could go wrong and result in something negative and ugly.

"God," I started praying in my mind, "if this is not the right time…"

Before I could even finish my prayer, Kenneth pulled back and said, "We'd better stop before we…before we…you know…before we…I want our first time to be…well, you know…I uh…" He was embarrassed! I felt he was a virgin, but now, with his hesitation, I am sure he is. I have never asked him, and he has never freely provided the information. Since I was not sure about this being the right time, I used his hesitation as an opportunity to deliver us both from our raging hormones.

"I can wait, if you want to wait." I said almost too calmly.

"I think that's best," he said and kind of let out a sigh of relief and continued to caress my shoulders and arms. "You see, I'm a Christian and I have always been taught that…"

"Kenneth," I interrupted him by putting my finger to his lips, "I'm a Christian too! We can wait!" At that point, we both let out a sigh of relief.

We kissed each other good night and went to our separate rooms. I was wide awake and unable to sleep, so I took another shower before preparing for bed. After my shower, I slipped into my red negligee. It was sexy, but not sleazy. I habitually set the alarm clock, turned off the light and got into bed.

I think I was asleep for about two hours when I felt myself awakening. After much tossing and turning, I decided I could not sleep anymore. I crept across the suite and found myself peeking into Kenneth's room. I could hardly breathe as I my eyes began to focus into the darkness of his room. He had the covers pulled up to his waist. I could see his chest moving up and down as he breathed. He must have felt me standing there because I heard his voice break into the silence from the dimly lit room.

"Can't sleep?" He asked, without moving his head.

"No, I can't"

"Would you like to sleep with me?" He lifted himself up on his elbows.

"May I?"

Without another word, he moved over towards the edge of the double bed as far as he could and lifted up the opposite side of the covers. I was all too happy to slip into the bed next to him. I laid there for a moment, next to him, with my head on his chest and my arm outstretched across his chest. He pulled me closer to him and I eased my bare thigh up onto his leg. I felt myself getting comfortable.

Then, I heard Kenneth make sounds as if he was clearing his throat as he moved around the bed a bit. He got out of the bed, motioning for me to stay where I was. I could see his dark colored, satin pajama pants as he moved around in the darkness. He separated the sheet from the comforter and slid in between them, forming a barrier between our bodies. I don't know if I was angry because I couldn't put my leg on top of his or if I was relieved because he was keeping us from sinning against God.

Even though I couldn't feel his body next to mine the way I wanted, I was still able to lie down on his chest with my arm outstretched across his chest. I could feel his chest underneath the palm of my hand and could hear his heart

76

beating. I felt his chest rise and fall as he breathed. Soon, I realized my breathing was in sync with his. I thought he was asleep until I heard him speak.

"I like the way this feels," he said in a sleepy voice. I smiled in agreement. We both fell into deep sleeps.

The next morning, the alarm rang. Instinctively, I reached over and turned it off. Gradually my mind and body began to merge and become one again. I opened my eyes slowly. The surroundings were so familiar.

I bolted up from my bed as my eyes filled with the familiar surrounding of my own bed room and the memories of the events from last night flooded back into my mind.

"Kenneth!" I said, frantically. I was expecting him to call me. The sunshine filling my room made me realize that the entire night passed and I did not hear from Kenneth. I looked towards the phone on the nightstand next to my bed. Horrified, I realized that the phone was off the hook! That must have happened when I hung up after calling the hotel!

I sat back down on my bed and beat myself in the head with my fist, as if to inflict some self punishment on me for being so stupid. I deserved everything that is happening to me, I reasoned to myself. Tears filled my eyes as I realized again, that I might loose Kenneth forever, with all of this foolishness in my life. I realized again a truth and reality. My dream was shattered.

I didn't want to be defeated, so I picked up the note from my nightstand and dialed the number to the Plaza Hotel, hoping against hope that Kenneth was still there. The phone rang.

"Good morning. Plaza Hotel, may I help you?" the voice on the other end asked.

"Do you have a room for Kenneth Williams?" I asked.

"Hold please while I check," the voice responded. There was a click and the sound of classical music filled my ear as I waited impatiently for the receptionist to return to the phone.

77

"No, ma'am. Mr. Williams checked out this morning," the voice said, not realizing how devastated I was to get the news. I hung up the phone without any additional conversation with the receptionist.

I looked out my bedroom window, trying hard to hold back the additional tears that were building up in my eyes. It was Sunday morning. I did not feel up to going to church. I walked to the living room and peeked out the window. Remo's truck was gone. He must have picked it up during the night.

I returned to my room and retrieved the lavender rose from the top shelf in my closet. It was wilted. I didn't want to loose it forever, so I went to the kitchen and carefully sealed it inside of two pieces of waxed paper, with some tape. Then I placed the rose and the note from Kenneth on top of the mementos in my keepsake box. After wiping the tears from my eyes and clearing the large knot from my throat, I tucked my secret box away, deep within my closet.

Chapter 12

LIFE IS A ~~PRISM~~ PRISON

*T*he days that followed seemed to blend together. My work was routine and my duties did not take much effort for me to perform. I didn't want to think about Kenneth because I didn't want to get depressed all over again about San Antonio. I convinced myself that Kenneth must be upset with me because I had not heard from him since I saw him last, at Ms. Dee's. I was so sure that he never wanted to see me again that I convinced myself not to call him, email him or write him any letters.

I was still sulking about the fact that Remo interfered with my dream weekend with Kenneth. It seemed as if Remo always knew how to make me more miserable. My thoughts and dreams were disrupted by the voice of one of my students.

"Ms. West, I can't find my name on this list," he said.

I'd made a sign in sheet for my class. This made it easier for me to check attendance. It was also a security back up for me. I wanted to make sure that someone was not responding for another individual when I called the roll.

"Let me see that," I said.

There were 15 names on the list, with 13 signatures. I asked the student, "What's your name?"

"Thomas," he replied, giving me his last name only.

I quickly observed his name as being the first one of the two remaining empty spaces on the list. I pointed to his name on the clipboard, held it approximately four inches from his face, and said sarcastically, "Woop! D'ere it is!" in one breath, making all of the syllables run together. All of the other students broke out into a hearty laughter. Thomas turned a deep shade of red, and signed his name on the list.

Working at the prison has taught me one thing. Life is like a prism. Life is full of colorful people, from all walks of life, with different problems, different circumstances and backgrounds that cause them to end up where they are, and so much more. With every turn of the prism there is a different set of colors. With every turn of a new day, there is a different set of people, problems and circumstances.

Everyday, my students entertained me with their colorful stupidity. If I could measure stupidity in degrees, some of my students would deserve Ph.D.s! One of my students was incarcerated for Burglary. He and his friends entered a private home during the Christmas holidays. They took the time to open the gifts that were under the tree before they left the home. One of the gifts was an instamatic camera. They loaded it with the film and commenced taking pictures of themselves holding up the gifts! That was stupid, but what makes them earn the Ph.D. is the fact that they left the pictures on the fireplace mantel to develop completely. They left the house with their loot, but forgot to take the pictures with them!

Police officers don't have to go looking for a majority of the drug dealers in my class, because they stand on the street corners, trying to make their sells. They remind me of the old watermelon farmers who would come into our neighborhood, with their old trucks filled with melons. As they drove slowly down the street, they would yell out the window, "Watermelon! Get your ice cold watermelon," knowing full well that the watermelon they were selling was definitely not "ice cold".

"Ms. West, can I restrain you?" one of my students asked. His voice startled me.

"Can you *restrain* me? What are you talking about?" I asked.

"I need a lawyer and I was wanting to put you on restrainer." He answered, with this serious sort of semi-professional look on his face. I tried desperately not to laugh.

"First of all," I tried to be serious, "I'm not an attorney. And secondly, the word is *retain*, not 'restrain'. Got that?" I responded as I leaned forward onto my desk. The other students tried muffling their voices as they laughed.

Working in the prison can be a dangerous place. I always try to find the colorful moments that keep me laughing, and keep me interested in my job. Unfortunately, the colorful days were becoming fewer and farther apart. Working here was becoming more and more prison like.

The remainder of the day went on without incident. I managed to keep my mind clear of all distractions. I made it through my classes without any trouble, skipped lunch, and answered all of the written request slips I'd received.

Before long, it was 3:00, time to go. I gathered up my things and headed for the door. I took a deep breath as I entered the walkway. With my eyes focused on the gate ahead of me, I walked as quickly as I could to the exit. I don't like to be stopped while I am on the walkway, so I try to ignore the voices of offenders calling me.

"Ms. West, Ms. West!"

There was an offender on the walkway, in front of me. I reminded myself to keep walking, no matter what he asked. If I stopped for him, there would be several others who would line up behind him, wanting an audience with me also.

"How can I help you?" I asked, as I continued walking.

"May I have a brief word with you?" he asked, trying to be polite.

"You just did!" I kept walking. "That was real brief!" I kept walking. I turned my head back towards him. "Thank you for keeping it that way! Have a good evening!" I smiled politely at him, knowing I was being sarcastic. He continued standing there on the walkway, with his arms outstretched, with a look of confusion on his face. I made a mental note to get with him the following day.

"Clickety-click". The gate opened. I stepped through to the other side. Closing the gate behind me, I felt myself...breathe.

Chapter 13

BAM'S BIRTHDAY

Since it was Bam's birthday, I was eager to be leaving my job and on my way home. As we have celebrated for years, I planned to meet my friends at OJ's for dinner. After leaving work, I relaxed awhile, trying to occupy my time until it was time to go. I showered, watched a little TV and then started getting dressed. I styled my hair and made up my face. My attire for the evening was simple. I put on a pair of starched white jeans, a black silk tee shirt and a black blazer. I was not trying to be cute to impress anyone. There was no one in Austin who impressed me.

By the time I arrived, Bam, Marilyn and Patrice were already there. They had selected a booth near the dance floor. I promised myself to have a good time. I didn't want my facial expressions to provide any hint of how depressed I was.

"Hey, you guys!" I greeted them, trying to be cheerful. They all looked great! Especially Bam. She had on this red leather blazer, a white lacy tank top, a short—not mini—red leather skirt and red leather pumps. Her bare legs did not need any help dressing up the outfit. Patrice was dressed in a blur of soft purple and baby blue. She was wearing an outfit she'd obviously designed herself. The colors blended and were easy on the eyes. Her head wrap matched the outfit. I have not seen anything like a lot of the clothes that Patrice wears. Marilyn had on a nice pastel sage green suit that consisted of a long, duster type jacket and long skirt. Her colorful soft pastel blouse completed her outfit. I slid into the horseshoe shaped booth next to Patrice.

OJ's Place is one of the best places in town to go out and have a good time. I'm not talking about OJ's as in the football player, but OJ's as in Oliver John McQuade, the ex-professional basketball player from Austin. He had to retire from the game after several knee surgeries. After he retired from basketball, he had this restaurant and club built. He offered dinner and entertainment to appeal to almost any adult aged person.

It wasn't your regular sports bar or club. It has more of a dinner and dancing type of atmosphere. The audience was mature, not elderly or mature in age, just that group of people who don't like loud rap music. This was a more Jazz, and a 70's & 80's era music group. Not too fast, not too slow and you can understand the lyrics enough to sing along. OJ preferred this music over today's music because "it's more romantic and you can appreciate the words", he'd always say. Although the music was old, the décor was modern, fresh, bright and up-to-date.

We all enjoyed coming to OJ's because of the standard the club set. There were no "hoochie mommas", dressed in almost nothing, and there were no "gang-bangers", dressed in their hoodlum attire with their pants hanging below their butts. The dress code and behavior code were strictly enforced.

The music sometimes made you feel as if you were caught in a time warp, but at least, you didn't have to worry about being shot or a drug deal going down at the table next to you.

When you first walk into OJ's there is a large foyer with ceramic tiles on the floor. There is a counter where you can check your coat. A few steps up were the restrooms which were located behind a concealing wall. Past the restrooms and on the other side of a short wall, the club opened up into the restaurant and dance area. There are tables arranged on the upper level, to the left. There were more tables in the middle, close to the dance floor and several booths lined the wall on the right side of the dance floor.

On the opposite wall, on the other side of the dance floor, was a bar and the DJ's Booth. This is one place that Remo and his group have not been able to play. Off to one side, was the kitchen and on the other side there was a private party room.

I looked around the room and began to take in the atmosphere. The music filled the air and I started feeling like I wanted to let myself and my troubles go, and have a good time with my friends. I felt myself letting go and concentrating on celebrating with Bam on her birthday.

We ate our dinners which consisted of salads and grilled chicken. We had cheese cake and strawberries for dessert; it was Bam's favorite. We were sipping our beverages and talking in general when a couple, dancing on the floor, caught our eyes and our attention. The song was an old Earth Wind & Fire jam. The couple was dressed in white, dancing slowly, looking into each other's eyes. The woman had both of her hands caressing her husband's face (we could see the big ring) and he had his hands correctly placed on her hips. They swayed rhythmically, never loosing sight of each others eyes. They would swing out and in, in rhythm with the music. It seemed as if their moves were choreographed to perfectly match that particular song. We all let out a little sigh, when they kissed at the end of the song.

We realized we'd stopped talking and we all had our attention fixed on that couple. No doubt, we were all wishing we were the ones who were dancing with that man or another man just like him.

"I wish someone would look at me like that," Patrice finally confessed first.

"I just wish my husband would look at me like that," Marilyn joined in the confession.

"I just wish Kenneth...," I confessed, before I knew what I was saying. I hoped I'd stopped myself before anyone else heard me.

"Oh, yeah," Marilyn said, as her memory was refreshed by my reckless confession. "Kenneth came by the beauty shop a while back! What was that about?" Marilyn said with this look of accusation.

"Don't worry about it!" I almost shouted.

"Are you still day dreaming about him?" Patrice asked. "Girl, you have been dreaming about him since we first met him in Fort Worth! You need to let that go and get on with your life!"

I don't want to let him go. He is too much a part of me. Couldn't my friends see that?

"Well, Patrice, I don't see you doing any better with your choice in men!" I tried to get the focus of the conversation off of me. "Kenneth is everything I have dreamed about and prayed for! I asked God for a sign, and He gave it to me!"

"Then why are you still messing around with Remo?" Marilyn was getting too far into my business. I really tried to change the subject.

"Patrice, if you wanted a sign, in order to know who your life long mate would be, what would that sign be?" I asked, desperate to change the subject.

She thought for a moment before she said anything. "My perfect man would be someone who would love me even after I told him about all of my secrets," she said with her head down, as if she was ashamed of some secret she has not shared with us.

"What about you, Marilyn? And don't tell us you found the perfect man in Darius!" I said. We all broke into a serious girl moment filled with laughter.

"Girl, you are telling the truth!" Bam screamed. "I have not told any of you this, but one day, I was on my way to Marilyn's and I saw Darius running down the street, wearing a pink shower cap, one of Marilyn's floral house coats and a pair of pink house shoes!" Bam could hardly contain herself as she shared this story and relived the scene. We were all laughing and holding our sides, all of us except Marilyn, of course.

"Stop lying!" Marilyn defended Darius. It was obvious that once again, she was upset by something Darius has done.

"Okay, Okay! I'm sorry! I was just joking. You know I can't stand him!" Bam said, putting her hand on Marilyn's shoulder, trying to calm her down. We all stopped laughing after we saw how upset Marilyn really was.

After things settled back down, I tried again to steer the conversation into a more healthy direction.

"So, Bam, what kind of sign would you pray and ask God for?" I asked.

"Well, after my three failures, I think the only man for me would be an older, gentle man. So, my sign would be that this older, gentle man would come to me with a single red rose in his hand. The rose would have to be red because red roses are traditional, a sign of romance, a sign of maturity, a sign of..." her voice trailed off as if she was concentrating on her sign and perhaps, a prayer.

We were so involved in our conversation that we initially did not see OJ approach our table with... one red rose in his hand.

"May I have the pleasure of this dance, Ms. Bam?" he asked in his deep Barry White, baritone voice. We all looked up at him with our mouths open. We knew God answers prayer, but that was FAST!

"Uh, I guess so," Bam responded. She reached up to take his hand and he presented the rose to her. As she reached for the rose with her free hand, I could clearly see that it was shaking slightly. As she stood up and they went to take the dance floor, Bam looked back at us with a smile that I have not seen on her face for a long time.

We were all watching them closely, so much so that I did not notice who was standing next to our booth.

"Can I have a dance?" I looked up. It was Remo— standing there, grinning down at me with his temporary golden grill in his mouth! How did he know I was here? I wanted to hide! He was wearing his normal oversized, heavily starched jeans, but this time, they were belted, still below his butt, but belted. He had attempted to tuck his lime green colored tee shirt in, as it was kind of puffed out all around. It was apparent to me that he was trying to abide by the dress code, without being in dress code.

While I was looking up at him, I was trying desperately to think of a response. I knew any negative answer would cause him to cause a scene. Reluctantly, I accepted his request to dance. Marilyn and Patrice could clearly see the despair on my face.

He grabbed my hand and led me out to the floor. I dragged my feet a little, because I really didn't want to dance with him. That would mean he would have to put his hands on me!

He chose a spot near the middle of the floor, pulled me close to him, put my arms around his neck and his arms around my waist. I cringed. I knew that the only way I could make it through this song would be to pretend I was dancing with somebody else. So, I closed my eyes and let my mind relive my San Antonio fantasy. I could feel Kenneth's hands around me, I could feel his breath on my neck and the smell of his cologne was filling my nostrils.

"Oh, Kenneth…" I let out in a whisper.

"What you say, baby?" Remo's voice snapped me out of my dream. I was horrified at the possibility that he heard me!

"Nothing," I said, trying not to be nervous.

Remo was satisfied not knowing what I'd said. He put his head close to my face and started singing the song that was playing, in my ear, out of tune. The noise was as irritating as a cat clawing a chalkboard. I endured the suffering by humming the final bars to the song that was playing myself, trying to drown out Remo's voice in my ear.

Finally, the song ended! I quickly broke our embrace and made my way to the booth where my friends and I had been sitting, before Remo could ask for another dance. Remo followed me to the booth. When I turned to sit down, there he was.

"Well, I know you ladies are doing yo' girls' thing, so I guess I'll leave and let you have yo' fun. See you later, baby," Remo said. Then he leaned over to give me a kiss. I was glad that it was just a lip kiss and not a long kiss. I was also glad that he decided to leave.

For the rest of the evening, Bam danced with OJ, Marilyn and Patrice continued in conversation, and I tried not to think about Kenneth or Remo. Every once in a while we would ask each other why was Bam still dancing with OJ.

Chapter 14

BE STRONG

♥

*B*am's birthday and the evening out broke up the mundane week I was having. Without a doubt though, I was glad for the weekend and some time off.

It was Saturday night. I didn't really have any plans. I was just sitting around, watching the Saturday night line up on TV. The door bell rang. It was Remo. This time he was wearing a red tee shirt, black oversized, heavily starched jeans, and a pair of red suede boots.

"What are you going to do tonight?" he asked me.

"Why?" I asked. I hated the way he tried to run my life and set my agendas. He is not my boyfriend! "What does he want now?" I asked myself.

"I've got a gig tonight in Waco. I'm just making sure you are gonna be home tonight," he said.

I was not going to stay at home just because he was telling me to. "Well," I started, "I've got my own plans."

"You ain't going no where!" Remo shouted as he got up in my face and pointed his finger at me. "I want you to be here when I get back! I need to put my stuff in yo' garage!"

I have never been one to step down. My mother is a strong woman. My grandmother is a strong woman, and my aunt is a strong woman. I have been blessed to be surrounded by these strong women. I stood my ground. Even though Remo was huge in his build and I only weigh about 120 pounds, I was not backing down! And, he has his own garage to put his equipment in! I didn't know what he had up his sleeve, but whatever it was, I knew I was not going to like it.

"I have plans, I'm going out. You go ahead and worry about your gig in Waco. You don't want to be late!" I firmly stated. I walked to my bedroom and pulled out something to wear. I called Patrice on the phone and told her to call Marilyn and Bam. We were going to OJ's Place. I hung up the phone and started ironing my clothes. Remo came into my room.

"I said you ain't going no where," he shouted as he took three fast and heavy steps into my bed room and towards me. I thought he'd left.

Without thinking, I grabbed the iron cord from the socket with my left hand as I maintained my grip on the iron with my right hand. With some inner strength, and unknown expertise, I quickly wrapped the cord around my hand and the top part of the iron. I held my newly fashioned weapon up in the air, ready to beat Remo across what ever part of his body crossed over the ironing board first and landed in my personal space.

"And I said I was going out!" I shouted back, under the protection of that still very hot iron.

Remo backed off.

"You crazy, little girl!" Remo said as he left my room. Seconds later, I heard the door slam. Shortly afterwards, I heard his big truck leaving.

"Good riddance", I thought. I was shaking like a wet cat, but I continued getting dressed. The truth is, I really didn't want to hurt Remo. He has his good points. It's just that when we get around each other, bad points come forth from both of us. I know he is definitely not the one for me.

Chapter 15

MY ONE NIGHT STAND

*W*ith Remo out of town in Waco, I could go out with my friends and enjoy myself. After Patrice picked me up, we met up with Bam and Marilyn at O.J.'s Place. It was about 9:00 in the evening.

We found a table, close to the dance floor. We ordered appetizers and drinks (non-alcoholic, of course) and patiently waited for someone to ask us for a dance.

After what seemed like hours of waiting, Prince walked over to our table and introduced us to his friend, Anthony Jennings. Anthony Jennings was from Oklahoma and was in Austin, checking out potential basketball players for St. Thomas University. How he and Prince met? I don't know and I didn't care! Somewhere between "Oklahoma" and his green eyes, the words began to fade into the distance.

Anthony was gorgeous! He did not have that muscle man build, but he was absolutely gorgeous! From that rich, black, naturally curly hair on his head, down to the soles of his feet, that man was good to look at. He had a very light complexion which intensified the green color of his eyes. His face was smooth, with the exception of his thin mustache and the tiny v-shaped goatee underneath his bottom lip. His smile was blinding! And, he had dimples! On both cheeks! He was casually dressed in a light blue shirt, and a pair of black slacks. He looked like he stepped off the cover of one of those male model magazines! My mind reentered the present, drawn by an unfamiliar voice.

"Will you dance with me?" it was Anthony, but who was he talking to?

"What did you say?" I asked half to myself and half to Anthony. I was still trying to wake myself up.

"Will you dance with me?" I was finally able to focus on the voice and the hand that was stretched out before me.

"I'd love to," I said as I accepted the hand that was attached to Anthony. As I stood up from the table, I turned to my friends and stuck out my tongue. I could tell they were so green with envy and so disappointed that Anthony didn't ask either of them to dance first. However, Prince did ask Patrice to dance.

We danced the night away. Every woman in O.J.'s was staring at us! Well, they might have been staring at Anthony, or maybe staring at me being with Anthony. I mean, this guy was absolutely handsome. His looks were enough to captivate an audience. He should have been a professional model instead of a basketball scout. I really had to work at not staring at him so much while we danced!

I kept asking myself, "Why is he with me? Why did he ask me to dance? Did Prince say something to him, or did I land this one on my own?" Finally, I didn't care! All I know is that by the last slow dance, I was ready for whatever this guy wanted from me! I wanted him! Forget virginity! Forget everything! I wanted him! I was screaming in my head.

It was time to leave O.J.'s Place. Anthony walked me back to my table. My friends were gone! Don't panic, I thought. I quickly searched the restaurant, looking for Prince or any other familiar face in the crowd. I needed someone to take me home. I wasn't going to call a cab, and frankly, I didn't trust myself to be alone with Anthony. Anthony could obviously see panic growing on my face.

"If it's alright with you, I'll give you a ride home. I don't mind." I could hear in his voice that he was sincere. I accepted his offer.

"If you don't mind, I need to stop and get a bite to eat. I was so busy dancing with you that I forgot to stop long enough to eat."

I agreed. We stopped at one of those fast food restaurants. He held my hand as we entered the building. From the moment we walked into the restaurant, everyone in there was staring at us! Okay, they were staring at Anthony, trying to figure out why he was with me. I didn't care. Guess on, people! I shouted to myself.

He finished his meal. I only ordered a soft drink. I couldn't eat a thing. I was too nervous. After he finished, we left the restaurant and I directed him to my house. I knew that Remo would still be out of town, so I wasn't concerned about him waiting for me when I got home.

He walked me to the door. I invited him in. He sat on the sofa. I offered him a soft drink, which he accepted. As I was walking back into the living room, he asked, "Who is that guy in the picture?"

He was looking at a picture of Remo on the stereo stand. He was sitting in a chair, surrounded by two young ladies, from one of his gigs.

"The girl in the picture, the one on the right, is my ex-roommate, Shawanna", I lied. "I don't know who that guy in the picture is," I lied even more. I couldn't believe me! I was flushing my integrity down the drain for a possible interlude with Anthony. I gave him the soft drink. He took a few sips as I sat down beside him. He drew me closer to him and then he kissed me. I felt the excitement growing in my body! I wanted him!

Then, he drew back and looked into my eyes and brushed my hair back from my face with his hand. I could hardly maintain myself as he stared at me with those hypnotic green eyes.

"I've got to go," I heard him say softly. "It's getting late and I have a long day ahead of me," he continued. "I had a great time tonight, thanks to you."

I was at a loss for words. I frantically searched my mind to come up with the perfect thing to say to keep him there, without coming on too strong. No luck.

"Okay," came out of my mouth, without even thinking. I was unable to think of anything else to say or do, so I surrendered. Anthony stood up from the sofa, I followed. I walked him to the door, we said our goodbyes. He gave me one last kiss….

After I closed the door behind him, I jumped up and down like a two-year-old throwing a temper tantrum at a grocery store. I can't believe I let that live specimen of gentle masculinity get away!

I ran over to the window and looked out, hoping I still had time to run out after him and shout, "Come back! I want you! I'm a virgin!"

Too late, he was already gone. I could see the taillights of his car turning the corner. I sulked. I looked at the clock, it was 2 AM.

I was too excited – really excited, know what I mean, to go to sleep. Now, I understand why guys have to take a cold shower. After taking my cool shower, (I couldn't stand it being too cold), I laid across my bed, in my bath robe, thinking about what shoulda', woulda', or coulda' happened.

96

"Okay you goofy girl," I told myself, "Snap out of it! He's gone! You only wanted his flesh."

The truth is, that is all I wanted. I would have slept with him and not even given it a second thought! My mouth was still drooling.

"Okay, reality check!" I thought to myself. "Wake up! Reality check!" I thought louder.

Too many times young women like me, give themselves cheaply, to a good looking man. I didn't even know Anthony! When I really thought about it, I felt myself becoming sick. I was going to give the most valuable part of me over to this complete stranger. I would have wasted my most precious gift on someone I would probably never see again. This time, I was blessed because this man showed more integrity and restraint than I did.

I reached over to my night stand and grabbed my stationary pad and pen. I started writing a letter to the love of my life.

> *Dear Kenneth,*
> *I was just lying here thinking about you....*

I am such a liar! I am trying to get Anthony Jennings out of my mind! I really wanted him out of my mind! I knew that my attraction to him was merely a flesh thing. I thank God for delivering me once again from my own flesh and desires. The truth is, Anthony would have been my one night stand. Kenneth is the one I want to spend the rest of my life with. He is worth the wait. I really wanted, in my heart, to wait for Kenneth. Lord, help me to wait!

I continued with my letter, pouring out my heart to Kenneth until I fell asleep.

Chapter 16

OLD CRUSHES DIE HARD

*T*he alarm went off. I looked at the clock. It read 7:00 AM. I was so sleepy. I had to get up, though. Today was Sunday and I wasn't going to let anything keep me from going to church. I saw the letter I was writing to Kenneth. It was crumpled underneath my head. The pen was still in my hand. I reread the letter, crumpled it up more and tossed it in the trash. I was still feeling guilty because of last night. And besides, I didn't think Kenneth would read the letter if I'd sent it to him anyway.

I was already showered, so I started getting dressed. I brushed my hair into its regular style, kind of straight, parted and accented on the side, with the slightest curl on the ends. The curls fell nicely between my shoulder blades. I took the time to add a little make-up. I didn't do that often, but today, I did.

I reached into my closet and pulled out a black and white two piece suit. This was one of my favorite suits. The white double breast jacket was cut just right so that I didn't need a blouse underneath. The collar was trimmed in black and the sleeves were accented with black and gold buttons. The knee length skirt hugged my body and fit like a glove. I added a pair of black pumps and gold jewelry to my outfit.

I looked myself over in the full length mirror on the back of my bedroom door. "I look pretty good, today," I thought to myself. I sprayed myself with my favorite perfume, and left.

As I was driving down Interstate 35, for some reason, I didn't take the normal exit towards my church. Today, I nodded my head in agreement with myself; I'll go to Killeen, to my mother's church. She will be surprised and pleased.

I arrived in Killeen and made my way to the New Life Ministries Church, where my mother is a member. I looked at my watch. It was 10:45. Just in time. I made my way into the church, past the security type ushers. I saw my mother sitting near the front of the sanctuary, in her normal seat. I made my way towards her. I tapped her shoulder and eased on into the pew. She smiled and hugged me. She was glad to see me.

She held on to my arm throughout most of the service. I did everything I could to just stay awake! Last night was exhausting! I was still tired from the short amount of sleep that I'd gotten. Fortunately, even though I threw it away, after writing my letter to Kenneth, my mind was completely closed to any other thoughts about Mr. GQ—you know, Anthony What's-His-Name!

After church was over, I waited in the foyer for my mother to do whatever it was she had to do. She is a well respected leader of women in her church. I'm sure she was seeing to some important matter.

I turned to walk towards the restroom, and there he was! Sylvester Davis! Also known as, "Sly--The Quarter Back--Davis! My old high school crush—and his wife, Sheryl! The last time I saw him, I was much thinner than I am now, my teeth were still crooked, I wore a pair of ugly plastic framed glasses, I was dressed like a tom-boy, and my hair was always pulled back into a pony tail!

"Angela? Angela West? Is that you?" He asked. It was obvious that he was surprised not only to see me, but to see how *good* I looked. I was glad I took a few extra minutes getting dressed this morning.

"Yes, Sylvester! How are you doing?" I said proudly, as I reached my hand out to shake his.

I had the biggest crush on him when we were in high school! Every time he smiled at me--or in my general direction--I would go weak in the knees. Every one knew I had a crush on him, even he did. Everyone also knew that he'd dated Sheryl since they were in junior high school and they planned to get married.

When we were seniors in high school, suddenly, Sylvester showed an interest in me. He asked me to go out to the lake with him for a picnic. I assumed he'd broken up with Sheryl so I was excited to accept his offer. My friend, Dora tried to stop me, telling me that he and Sheryl were still together, but I wouldn't listen.

After we arrived at the lake, his true intentions were revealed. He made sexual advances towards me! My excitement turned to horror! I was ashamed that I was so gullible as to believe that he actually had feelings for me, so quickly after he ended his four-year-long, relationship with Sheryl. Fortunately for me, when I firmly told him "no", he respected my wishes and took me home.

Needless to say, after I returned to school from the *date*, I learned that he was, in fact, still dating Sheryl, he had no intentions of breaking up with her, and she didn't know about our date at the lake. I realized that I would have been his one-night-fling-thing, and Sheryl would still be his virgin bride. I wanted so much to tell her but Dora convinced me that nobody would believe me and he wasn't worth it anyway.

All I can say is I eventually lived down the guilt and shame that I felt. I had not spoken to him again, since that day, until now. Today, however, I felt victorious as I looked at him and Sheryl. He didn't look as good now as he did in high school. He had picked up a few pounds. His belly was hanging over his belt and his hair line was receding!

He was standing there with Sheryl and their four children ranging in ages 8 years to about 18 months. The youngest of the four children was sitting on Sheryl's hip, as she was hanging on to him, to keep him from falling. The oldest one, their daughter, was rather plump and looked like a miniature Sheryl.

"So, tell me! How are you two doing? You have been together since high school! Sylvester, did you get that football scholarship and go to college like you dreamed?" I was full of questions because I really wanted to know.

"No, I didn't go to college. Sheryl got preg..." Sylvester said, looking back over his shoulder at his wife, "I mean, Sheryl and I decided to get married right out of high school and I just haven't had the time to go".

"Well, it's never too late!" I honestly tried to encourage him! "What are you doing for yourself?" I asked, not out of concern, but out of nosey curiosity.

"I'm a uh...I uh...I'm a Diesel Engine Specialist," he finally said. I guess that meant he was working at either a gas station or some auto repair shop. I remember how he hated to get his hands dirty.

"What about you, Sheryl? I remember you were always talking about being a doctor." I could hardly contain myself as I smiled at them. My smile was there as a silent voice of triumph! More than likely, when I refused to be used, he pressured Sheryl just enough to convince her to sleep with him before they were married. That could have been me, there, with Sylvester.

"Well, I'm a house wife and I like what I do, making my man happy and taking care of our children", she said as she grabbed Sylvester's arm, trying to convince me of how happy she was. I could tell she was lying. The baby on her hip started whining and I could tell Sheryl was getting frustrated, trying to keep the baby quiet so that she could hear the conversation between Sylvester and me.

"Are you married?" he asked me.

"No, not yet. I guess I just haven't met the right man yet," I said proudly. I wanted him to know that he is not, was not and never will be, the right man for me. I wanted to tell him about my "fiancé", Kenneth and how successful he is and how much in love with me he is, but lately, I have been reaping the negative benefits of my "untruths", so I thought it best to speak only the truth.

"Remember that day at the lake?" I asked, trying to stir his memory.

"The lake?" he asked.

"Yeah, you know," I continued, "you and I, well, we almost, I mean…"

I could see the look on his face grow from confusion as he was trying to remember, to embarrassment as the memory became clear in his mind. I just smiled as he desperately changed the subject.

We continued to stand in the foyer, making light conversation, until my mother emerged from one of the offices nearby. She motioned for me to leave with her. I was all too eager to leave.

"Well, see you guys later! Bye kids! Nice to meet you!" I gave a vigorous wave goodbye and walked towards the exit, still feeling victorious for not falling into the "trap".

Young people get "trapped" when they play sexual roulette. They end up getting pregnant much earlier than they plan and their futures are altered forever. I'm glad that my future is still being written. I may not be married right now, but all of my options are still open and my opportunities are still available. My life has not been complicated by children I am not ready to be a mother to.

As I was leaving out of the church, I could hear Sheryl asking, "What was she talking about? What day at the lake? What were you doing at the lake with her? When did this happen?"

"Drop it, Sheryl!" he snapped at her. The baby started crying again.

As the church door closed behind me I felt I was leaving with my regained dignity. I threw up my hand in triumph! For a long time, I was wondering about the "one that got away"! Now, I was glad I didn't have to wonder anymore! The feelings that I had for that old high school crush were definitely dead!

Chapter 17

"SHADY GRADY"

♥

*I*t was another Saturday. I found myself at Ms. Dee's. I was the one who came in early.

I checked my hair to make sure it was dry. Ms. Dee would send you back to the dryer room if your hair wasn't dry completely. My hair was dry, so I left the dryer room. As I exited the dryer room, I ran into "Shady" Grady.

Actually his name was Herman Grady. Everybody called him "Shady" not because his business dealings were questionable but simply because it rhymed with Grady and it was better than calling him Herman! Shady was Ms. Dee's supply man. Every Friday he would bring hair care supplies to the shop. Every once in a while, something would happen or come up to prevent him from coming on Friday. When that happened he would show up on Saturday.

Grady was one of those guys who would just get on your nerves! He was about 34 years old, only about 5 feet tall, overweight, has a curl on what's left of his hair, and one gold tooth in the front of his mouth, surrounded by his other stained and decaying teeth. He has this irritating way of sucking on that one gold tooth all the time! He spoke with a whine of a voice that would just grate against your nerves.

"Oh, excuse me, baby," he said sucking on that tooth. "I didn't see you there". He paused, I tried walking away, but he grabbed my arm. "Say baby," he calls every lady "Baby", except Ms. Dee.

"I sho' wish I was going wit' chew, baby!" he said as he backed up towards me, shaking his leg in what I guess was suppose to be a tantalizing fashion.

"My, my! You sho' looks good to me! You could be a fried chicken leg swimming in a plate of gravy!" Now, he was sucking and picking that one gold tooth with a toothpick.

He sniffed the air, "Girl, you smell so good, I could bottle you up and sell you fo' air freshener," he continued to flirt. "How about you and me goin' out tonight! I am the man that will make you forget cho' troubles".

"Look you little creep! Get your greasy hand off of me with your country-fied, no-good, ain't-had a-date in a long time, need to be spaded, tired scary curl wearing, stuck on stupid self," I said—well, that's what I wanted to say.

But instead, and to my mind's surprise my mouth quickly formed the words, "Okay, I'll go out with you. Meet me at OJ's Place about 8:00 this evening."

"Alright then, baby," he chuckled; half believing I was going to go out with him.

He was right to wonder! There was no way I was going to keep that date with him! At least that was what my mind was trying to convince me of.

Without trying or wanting to, my mind kept visualizing his half-hairy chest sticking out of his half buttoned shirt. His shirts always looked two sizes too small and he always leaves the top three buttons open. "What, is he trying to turn somebody on with that pork belly chest?" I asked myself.

"Yuck!" I said out loud making a face and shaking as if I was trying to let go of a bad taste in my mouth. I walked back to Ms. Dee's station so she could finish my hair.

"*SLAP!*"

I heard the horrible sound of skin hitting skin! I looked back over my shoulder towards the door. There was Bam, dressed to the 9's, with her hands on her hips, looking very disturbed and looking down at Grady. Shady Grady was standing there with his mouth open and his hand on his cheek.

"You horrible little man!" she said in an almost too proper voice! Shady Grady must have said something to her that she did not like. Tossing her head up, Bam spun around towards Ms. Dee's booth. She didn't wait for Grady to apologize. Her face was still frowned up in anger. All of the men in the barber area laughed at Shady Grady, telling him that he should have known better than to talk to Ms. Bam the way he talked to me. They were right!

Chapter 18

THE DATE

♥

I walked back to Ms. Dee's booth, trying to forget that I'd told Shady Grady that I would go out with him. The truth is, I just didn't like him! But, with all of the drama I have been going through with Remo, and the loneliness I have been feeling because of Kenneth, I just needed something to get my mind off of my troubles.

"Girl, I know I didn't just hear you make a date with Shady Grady!" Kiki said as she followed me, pressing for a confession. Obviously, she'd been listening to our conversation, from her station near the dryer booth. Kiki was always in other people's business.

"If I did Kiki, that is my business!" I defended myself.

"You know he is no good! Every time he comes here on Saturday, he stays the night at a hotel, hoping to get lucky with whatever hoochie momma he can get! Ya'Shika even went out with him!" she continued her argument.

"Don't worry about it! I' m not going out with him anyway. I just said that to get him to leave me alone." I said. Actually, I said I would go out with him because I was feeling so sorry for myself. I was telling myself that I did not deserve someone like Kenneth, and I didn't want anyone like Remo. Who's left? Shady Grady.

Kiki threw her hands up in defeat and disgust, feeling as if her argument fell on deaf ears. I heard her loud and clear. I already knew what kind of man Shady was.

Ms. Dee finished my hair. When I had left the salon, it was about 3 in the afternoon. With no specific plan, I busied myself running errands and shopping for groceries. By the time I made it home, it was 6:30pm. As soon as I walked inside, I was overcome with guilt. My mind was bombarded with statements about Shady and meeting him for dinner.

"But now, I don't want to go!" I shouted to myself.

The time I spent riding around, gave me time to think and clear my head. Maybe I didn't deserve Kenneth, for sure I didn't want Remo, but God knows, and now I know too, that I don't have to settle for SHADY GRADY!

I argued with myself until finally, my conscience and good heart won over, so I prepared myself for the worse that could happen. If he got too out of line, I wanted to be prepared to kick him, beat him down, and run, if I had to.

I put on a white tank top. On top of that, I put on a pink, button down, oxford shirt, making sure all of the buttons were closed. Then I slipped into a pair of panty hose and put my freshly starched blue jeans on over them. After making up my face, I finished my look with a brown leather belt, a pair of burgundy, low heeled boots, and my favorite burgundy leather blazer.

All during the drive to OJ's, I kept going over some scenarios in my head, pre-planning my escapes. I finally arrived at OJ's, about fifteen minutes late. I hoped he had already been there and left. I looked around the restaurant, as I was holding my breath. Not only was I hoping he was gone, but

I was also hoping that there was not anyone at OJ's that I knew, just in case Grady was there.

Unfortunately, I spotted him, sitting at a table out in the middle of the restaurant where everybody could see him. I wanted him to sit at a booth where I could hide. He was putting cocktail olives on his finger tips and then eating them off. Although he'd changed his shirt, the shirt that he had on was still too small, unbuttoned, and now, he had three gold chains and a huge silver medallion hanging around his neck!

"I can still leave", I thought, "He hasn't seen me!" I turned to leave.

"Hey Baby," I heard him shout, "Here I am!" I turned back towards him and saw that he was waving his hands in the air trying to get my attention, as if yelling in this fine restaurant like someone who grew up in the country wasn't enough.

Reluctantly, I walked over to his table. I sat down and quickly explained to him that I had already eaten and all I wanted was something to drink. The waitress came over to the table to take our orders.

"This will be separate tickets," Shady said, before the waitress could even ask.

"Stupid and cheap," I thought to myself, "Let's just get this over with."

Grady ordered the "fried chicken plate". Who comes to a place like OJ's and orders fried chicken? A fried chicken plate was not even on the menu! However, after an extremely loud discussion with the waitress, she agreed to have the cook take the chicken from the Baked Chicken plate and "throw some flower and milk on it and fry it up in some grease," as Grady demanded.

I was so embarrassed! I tried to hide my face from the people who were staring at us.

"And what would you like to drink, sir?"

Don't say it, Grady!" I was saying to myself. All the time while he was placing his order, I had my elbows on the table and my head down in my hands, shielding my face from the waitress. I knew Shady just wasn't going to do right.

"I'll have a 40 oz. bottle of yo' finest…"

"We don't sell 40 oz's here. All we have is draft," the waitress interrupted Shady.

"Draft? I ain't trying to join no army or nuthin' like that. I just want some beer!" He slapped his leg and started laughing so loud, I thought he purposely made his ordering blunder under the pretense of making a joke. Neither the waitress nor I was amused.

The waitress just looked at me as if to say, "Is he for real?"

I looked at her and just shook my head.

"Just bring me what you got," Shady finally said.

I ordered two virgin strawberry margaritas. I wanted enough to drink to keep my mouth busy without having to communicate with him. When the waitress brought our drink orders, she brought 4 drinks to me.

"I only ordered 2", I said.

"Tonight is ladies night, you get two for one," the waitress explained.

"You sho' you gonna drink all that? You might get a little tipsy!" Grady chuckled, sucking on that gold tooth.

I could see in his devious little eyes that he wanted me to get a "little tipsy" so he could take advantage of me. But, he didn't realize that a virgin drink comes without alcohol. The only thing that was going to get me tipsy was that intoxicatingly nauseous odor coming from his mouth. I looked at him in disgust, rolled my eyes, and then looked up to the ceiling as if I was calling out to God.

"Let's just get this over with!" I shouted to myself.

While we were waiting for his meal, Grady mentioned there was something in his shoe. Before I could say anything, he took his shoe off and put it on the table! His sock had a big hole and his big toe was sticking out. He had his foot resting on his knee, massaging his toes! Then he put his fingers to his nose and took a sniff! I wanted to throw up! Of course, he didn't wash his hands before he ate and he didn't wipe the table off when he removed the shoe.

Finally, Grady's dinner arrived and he kept himself busy eating his chicken with his hands and sucking the grease from his fingers. I looked up over my second margarita when he leaned back in his chair, gave a loud burp and started picking his teeth with the fingernail on his pinky finger.

About another thirty minutes into the "date", Grady asked me to dance. I'd just finished my second drink and was working on the third. There was a slow song playing. I quickly imagined Grady on the dance floor, dancing up to me, trying to grab onto me, and trying to feel on my body! The vision just made me sick to my stomach! His greasy little grubby hands feeling on me! I could not bear the thought.

The next thing I envisioned was a fast song playing and Grady asking me to dance. I saw myself very embarrassed by the chicken like dancing Grady would be doing. Then he started doing something that resembled the Tick, Penguin and the Hammer Dance all mixed up together. I shuddered at the thought and realized I had to come up with a reason not to dance with him at all.

"No, thank you. I'm already feeling a little, you know, tipsy," I said calmly, putting two fingers from my left hand to my temple, trying to make my excuse seem more convincing. Grady winked his eye at me, chuckled a bit, sucked on his tooth, and put a few more bites of his fried chicken in his mouth.

I felt myself grieving as Grady started talking about his climb to the top in the hair care product supply business. I excused myself to the restroom. While I was in the restroom, I started arguing with myself about leaving. Since the restrooms were located in the front, I could leave without him seeing me. I reasoned I could tell him later on that I got to the restroom and threw up, so I had to leave. Then I convicted myself again for swaying from the truth. I really had to work on the truth thing.

After spending a few relaxing moments in the restroom, I decided I would just leave. But, to my surprise, when I opened the restroom door, Grady was standing in the archway which led to the hall where the restrooms are located. Fortunately, his back was to me. I closed the door to regroup before I opened it again. When I opened the door the second time, Grady was still standing there, but now he was making obscene gestures with his hands and his pants. I closed the door a second time to regroup.

When I reopened the door again and saw Grady still standing there, I decided to go ahead and exit the restroom. Grady said he came to the restroom because he knew I was "loaded" and might need his help to get back to the table. He didn't want me to get lost or to fall down. I thought it best just to remain silent.

Two hours later, my drink glasses were empty. Grady was still going on and on about how he was going to "rock" my "world". He is so stupid.

Finally, I asked a question that I somehow already knew that answer to, "Are you married?" I leaned onto the table, maintained a straight face, and put my elbows on the table to stress my seriousness.

Hesitantly, Grady shook his head and replied, "No, I can't seem to find the right woman. You available?" He asked his question with an insecure laugh attached to it.

"No, I'm not available and I don't think I'm your type," I stated rather frankly. "You have kids though, don't you?"

Now he was really ashamed, as he nodded his head in affirmation. I was ready to go. I was not going to ask him how many children or with how many different women.

"I'm leaving," I said as I stood up from the table. Somehow, my hand slipped when I grabbed the edge of the table to stand, and I fell back into the chair. I laughed at myself.

"Ooh, Baby!" I could hear excitement building in Grady's voice. "You can't leave in that condition! You need me to drive you home!"

Grady thought I was drunk. Now what do I do? I didn't want him to drive me home, and I didn't want him to follow me either! Quickly I devised a plan.

"What hotel are you staying in?" I asked.

"I ain't checked into one yet. I was planning to go to the one right down the street," he lied as he was sucking on that tooth again.

Right down the street, I thought. This just might work. We paid our separate checks and got up from the table. He grabbed me and held onto me as if he was trying to keep me from falling, since I was, you know "tipsy". He smelled of chicken grease, beer and stale cologne.

We arrived at the hotel. He checked in, while I waited in his rusty gray Toyota. He kept his eye on me as he checked into the room. I continued to work on my plan. A few minutes later, he parked the car closer to the door and he ushered me into his first floor room. It was dimly lit with only the bed lamp being turned on. He helped me lay down on the bed. Almost immediately, he began trying to remove my clothes by taking off my jacket. When he realized he was not succeeding, he tried to take off my pants by loosening my belt. I rolled over onto my stomach, with my arms underneath me, and pretended to be semi-passed out. He kept trying to figure out how to get into my clothes, with me laying on all of the buttons and zippers.

Finally, he gave up on me and started working on himself. I saw him take off his pants and shirt. He was wearing boxers, white boxers. I hate boxers, especially the white ones! I could see him, as I was peeking through my eyelashes. He walked over to the mirror, and did a self check. He tested his breath, smelled underneath his arms, and looked into the front of his boxers.

"What is he doing?" I asked myself. "Does he think it's going to disappear or something?" I tried to keep from laughing.

113

I saw him rummage through his overnight bag; he removed toiletries and a clean pair of white boxers from the bag and went into the bathroom. I heard the shower running. This is my chance! I got up from the bed and ran out! I ran all the way back to the restaurant and got into my car.

In the safety of my car, I laughed when I imagined Shady Grady's face after he'd gotten out of the shower and saw that I was gone. I'd left the door to his room wide open.

During the drive home, I couldn't help but think about how immature and dangerous my actions were. I should have just told Grady I did not want to go out with him. No, I should have told Remo... No, I wouldn't even wish that fate worse than death on Grady.

I made a mental promise to myself never to do anything like that again!

Chapter 19

WHITE BOXERS

*T*he alarm rang. I turned it off. It was 4:30, Thursday morning. The past weekend was still on my mind. That Saturday night with Shady Grady was a disaster. Sunday passed as usual. I prayed my way through another Sunday service.

My work week was routine and mundane. The same old thing, the same old offenders, this prism was becoming more boring and unsatisfying. Once again, it was Thursday and it was time for me to get up and get ready for work. I rolled over to get out of bed, trying to remember what I had been dreaming the night before. Oh, I remember. My pillow was wet. Obviously, I'd been crying in my sleep. Kenneth, again, I thought to myself. God, help me!

I got up and went to my closet. I pulled out my keepsake box. There, on top of my many cards and letters from Kenneth was the one single, lavender rose, pressed between two pieces of waxed paper. The sealed edges were helping to keep my precious memento from loosing its luster too quickly. I dried my now teary eyes, replaced the rose back into the box, and prepared myself for work.

As I arrived at the prison unit, an eerie feeling crept over me. It was almost as bad as the feeling I would get when Remo was close. After working at a prison for a while, your senses become more intense. This is one of those feelings you get when something just isn't right. I promised myself to be extra cautious today.

It wasn't long after I entered into the facility that I learned my feelings were warranted. The unit was on lockdown status. This is when all activity has been canceled. All of the offenders have been remanded to their bunks and housing locations. The cafeteria is closed, school is closed, the recreation yards are empty and the medical department is open for extreme emergencies only. Everything is halted. It almost looks like a ghost town.

The reason for the lockdown was simple. Over the weekend, officers received information about drugs being in the facility. The initial search resulted in a gallon bag of marijuana and a homemade weapon being found in one of the dormitories. After the first finding, several offenders began providing more information about other drugs that were on the unit. At that point, the unit was locked down so that a person-by-person, cell-by-cell, inch-by inch search could be conducted. Although it meant I would not have to teach my class today, I was still uncomfortable. My mind kept shifting back and forth between Shady Grady and the incident over the weekend, my high-school crush, my increasing feelings for Kenneth, and some feelings and incidents in my past that I would rather soon forget—forever!

I decided to take off early, since the day had progressed and the lockdown had not been lifted. Unfortunately, I chose the wrong moment to walk out of the facility. There on the walkway were about twenty offenders, all striped down to their boxers, white boxers. They were all lined up, waiting for

116

officers to search their clothes before they were allowed to dress.

This was the process. The ranking officers would designate the next area to be searched. The officers would perform visual body searches of those confined to the area and send them outside in their boxers until their clothes could be searched. After searching the clothes, the offenders were allowed to get dressed, but had to remain on the walkway until the search of the living quarters was complete.

I tried not to look at them! I really did not want to see them! Too many emotions! Too many memories! People have always teased me because I walk so fast when it is time for me to leave this place. I just don't want to see any white boxers!

I quickly headed for the gate. Despite my efforts against it, my mind shifted back to when I was seven years old. At that time, with my father, being in the military, my family was stationed at the military base in Frankfurt, Germany. We lived in a military apartment complex with other military families. Life was simple.

My best friend, Monica, asked if I could spend the night with her. My mother gave her permission. "This will be fun," I thought to myself. After my mother packed up my clothes for the night, Monica and I walked the short distance between our apartment and hers.

Monica announced to her mother that I had arrived. She came out of the kitchen and gave me a hug, making me feel very welcomed. Monica's family consisted of her mother and father, and her three older brothers. I don't know how old her parents were but, I believe they were much older than mine. Her father had salt and pepper hair and her oldest brother, as far as I can remember, was already out of high-school.

Monica's room was so pretty! Everything was so pink! Everything matched; the curtains, the bed, even the throw rugs on the floor! I sat my bag of clothes down on the floor near the bed and sat down on the fluffy pink comforter.

"Get up! Get up!" Monica cried in a panicky whisper, "Get off the bed! Nobody is allowed to sit on the bed with the spread on it!"

I thought to myself that it was strange that her mother did not allow anyone to sit on the bed. I stood up from the bed and continued to look around. As beautiful as it was, I realized this room was missing something—toys! There were no toys in this room! No dolls, no games, no dishes, no nothing! That was almost too strange!

Monica and I went back into the living room. She pulled a book off of a shelf and laid with it on the floor. From the chair where I was sitting, I could see that the book was full of pictures. Then I realized there was no TV. Monica looked up at me. I cold tell she was about to invite me to lay on the floor with her and look at the book. But, before she could ask, her father came over to her, making loud laughing noises and said to her, "I'm going to tickle you!"

Monica started screaming with laughter even before the tickling began. She was squealing with laughter and rolling all over the floor. Her middle brother came over and "helped" her father tickle her. They were laughing so loud. Strange.

Monica's father looked up at me and invited me to participate in this "tickling game".

"No, thank you," I politely declined. For some reason, I just didn't like the way Monica's father and her brother were "tickling" her. It was strange to me and I knew I didn't want anybody to tickle me like that. I cringed at the thought.

Monica's mother called from the kitchen, letting all of us know that it was time for dinner. I could hardly eat. That "tickling" thing was still on my mind. I asked myself why she let her dad tickle her like that. I just didn't understand.

"My daddy would *never* tickle me like that! I wouldn't *want* my daddy to tickle me like that! And my brother—if he would try to tickle me like that, I would just punch him in the face, even if he is older and bigger than me!" I continued to think to myself.

We either ate dinner in silence or I was so deep into my thoughts that I failed to hear any of the conversation going on at the dinner table.

After dinner, Monica and I were finally able to enjoy the book she'd chosen earlier. It was full of beautiful pictures of sea creatures. As we began to submerge ourselves into fantasies about living under the ocean, I continued to keep an eye on Monica's father's whereabouts. I didn't want him to come up behind me and tickle me.

Sometime later, Monica's mother indicated it was time for us to take a bath. I gathered my nightclothes and entered the bathroom. As I was trying to close the door, Monica came in behind me with her nightclothes in her hand. A look of confusion crossed my face.

"We're gong to take a bath together!" she giggled. At first I wanted to resist, but, I thought, this will be all right. My fears were soon drowned in that huge mountain of bubbles Monica's mother had prepared for us!

We stayed and played in those bubbles so long, Monica's mother had to make us get out! Reluctantly, I pulled the plug, as Monica got out of the tub and dried off. I was playing with the last few bubbles as they slid down the drain, when I looked up and saw something that really caught my attention. Monica put on her pajamas without any panties! I'd never seen that before!

Without mentioning my confusion, I got out of the tub, dried off and tried to hide the fact that I was putting my panties on from Monica. I didn't want her to think something was wrong with me.

We went into Monica's room and got into her twin bed. Her mother had already removed the fluffy pink comforter, folded it, and placed it on a chair near the bed. Monica allowed me to take the inside side, and she took the outside. The outside was closest to the bedroom door. Monica's mother gave us both a kiss on the forehead, turned out the light and exited the room, closing the door behind her. It was dark. Monica and I talked and giggled until we drifted off to sleep.

Sometime during the night, the sudden light that flooded into the room awakened me. Rubbing my eyes, I tried to focus. There, standing in the doorway, illuminated by the hall light, was Monica's father, Mr. "X" (he doesn't deserve a name). He was standing there, leering into the room, with nothing on but a pair of white boxers. I could see his fat belly hanging over the elastic waist band on the boxers.

Without shutting the door, he came over to the bed. His heavy breathing, and his body weight pressing against the bed, stirred Monica. "Hi, Daddy," she said, barely lifting her head from her pillow.

He started "tickling" Monica again, only this time, she wasn't laughing. I stared in horror! I saw his huge hand coming towards me! I wiggled and squirmed as much as I could to get away from his hand! I didn't want to be "tickled"!

"Didn't he know that"! I shouted to myself. I was fighting so hard to get away from that huge hand, but I had no place to go. The wall was behind me and Mr. "X" was in front of me. I couldn't scream! I was so glad I had my panties on.

"Jesus, help me!" I prayed silently. "Stop it!" I heard myself say to him, in a shouting whisper.

Suddenly, Mr. "X" stopped and stood up. I looked at him. Unfortunately, the only thing I could see clearly through my tears was his white boxers and the "thing" that was protruding out of the opening of his shorts. I shielded my eyes, trying to forget what my young, innocent eyes had just seen.

"You saw his 'thing'!" I kept condemning myself.

Mr. "X" left the room, closing the door behind him. Monica had drifted back to sleep. I couldn't sleep. I kept replaying the incident over and over in my head. I cried.

"This family is so strange!" I kept thinking.

The next morning, Monica's mom came into the room and cheerfully ordered us to get dressed for breakfast. I didn't want breakfast.

"We need to pray," I told Monica after her mother left the room and we dressed.

"Why?" she asked.

"Because we sinned!" I replied. "And we need to ask Jesus for forgiveness because I don't want to go down to the devil!" Now, I was crying and shouting.

I really could not explain to Monica or myself what was wrong or why we needed to pray. All I knew is that what happened last night was wrong and somebody needed to ask for forgiveness. Since I felt so badly, obviously I am the one who needed to do the asking. Gathering up my courage to go before God, I kneeled down next to Monica's bed, I bowed my head and with my hands folded together in prayer fashion, I began to pray. Monica joined me. I gathered up the most repentant prayer that I, as a seven-year-old could...

> *"Now, I lay me down to sleep,*
> *I pray the Lord, my soul to keep.*
> *If I should die before I wake,*
> *I pray the Lord my soul to take.*
> *If I should live another today,*
> *I pray the Lord will guide my way.*
> *Bless my Momma, bless my Daddy,*
> *Bless my brothers, and bless me.*
> *Amen, Jesus wept."*

Somewhere in that prayer was a statement of confession and a request for forgiveness, there just had to be. I was wiping my tears away from my eyes as quickly as I could, trying to keep the obvious fact that I was crying a secret. I failed miserably. The tears were coming too fast. I couldn't keep up.

I dressed myself and put all of my dirty clothes and other items back into the paper bag my mother had used to pack my things in. I rolled the top of the bag down. I wiped more tears away from my eyes.

Throughout this time, Monica was staring at me in disbelief. She couldn't understand why I didn't like Mr. "X"s tickling game. I told her I had to leave. I grabbed my paper bag and headed for the door, walking as quickly as I could. I didn't want to see Mr. "X" and I was hoping to get past Monica's mother who was busy in the kitchen. I didn't want her to see that I had been crying, and I didn't want her to ask me what the problem was. I knew I would not be able to explain.

Monica followed me, but couldn't keep up. I reached the door and fortunately, it was unlocked. I ran all the way home and went straight to my bedroom. Closing my bedroom door behind me, I dumped the dirty clothes from the bag onto the floor. I removed the panties I was wearing and put on a clean pair from my drawer. For some reason, the ones I had on felt extremely dirty. I put those panties into the paper bag and rolled the top back down again. I carried the bag to the kitchen and put it in the trash.

"Did you have fun?" my mother asked. She was in the kitchen, getting ready to prepare breakfast. I stared at her for a few moments. How can I explain that I didn't like being tickled? I searched my mind to try to find some words that could describe what happened to me. The more I thought, the guiltier I felt! If I told my mother about the tickling thing, I would have to tell her I sinned. Sin is bad! Sin makes people feel bad! I could not remember ever feeling more badly than I felt at that moment.

"It was okay," I finally responded.

"Clickety-click". I heard the gate open. I reached out to grab it and pulled it opened.

"I hate white boxers!" I muttered to myself as I walked through the gate and quickly closed it behind me.

Chapter 20

PICNIC FOR TWO

*A*fter I reached the outer door, I put on my sunglasses and looked up towards the sky. "It's a beautiful day," I said to myself.

"Toot-toot," I heard a car's horn and looked in the direction of the sound. I stopped breathing for a moment.

"Is it…?" I asked myself. "No, it can't be," I answered. I took a few steps towards my car. "Stop dreaming," I said out loud.

"Toot-toot". The car horn again. This time, I took my sunglasses off. When I turned to look, I could clearly see him standing next to his car.

"Kenneth," I said, letting out a half breathe. I wanted to just run over to him and tell him to take me away. But instead, I managed to maintain my composure as I walked towards him and his deep green, four-door Jaguar.

"Hi," I said, wanting to jump across his car, grab him up and take him home with me. He looked so good! His full beard was masterfully trimmed. His smile was mesmerizing. He was dressed in business attire, with a firmly starched, white shirt, taupe colored slacks, brown shoes and a tie that added just the right colorful accent.

The wind blew. I could smell his cologne. "Mmm, I could wake up next to this man every morning for the rest of my life!" I was thinking.

"Hey, Niecy!" his smooth voice caught my attention. He was the only one I know who calls me "Niecy". His voice pulled me away from my brief day dream. I could feel my teeth drying out from all of the smiling.

"What are you doing here?" I asked.

"Well, since I was unable to meet you in San Antonio, I thought I would try again to catch up with you by meeting you here for work. I had to come to Austin on business and managed to finish up early. I would have called but I didn't want to disappoint you if I was unable to finish my business in time enough to meet with you before I head back to Dallas. I figured you would be at work and I knew you would be leaving at some point today. So, I took a chance, came by and parked my car, just waiting to see you here. Would you mind joining me for a picnic?"

This time, I did jump across the hood of his car, grabbed him by his shirt, threw him down on his car, anchored my knee in his chest, leaned forward and forced my tongue into his unsuspecting mouth!

Okay, that's what I *wanted* to do. Instead, I politely accepted his offer. He came to the passenger's side and opened the door for me, revealing the tan interior of his Jag.

He wasn't kidding when he said picnic! There on the back seat was a picnic basket! I mean a *real* wicker picnic basket, checkered blanket and a bunch of wildflowers! He reached into the back seat, grabbed the flowers and presented them to me.

"These are for you," he whispered. I smiled and graciously accepted them. He leaned forward, we shared a kiss. He took my hand and helped me into his car.

"Where are we going?" I was almost afraid to ask.

"It's a surprise," he replied, flashing that perfect smile.

We drove to a part of Austin that was new to me. Throughout the drive, we made small talk. He let me know that he had been promoted to Regional manager for his office. He's still single, and "waiting on the right woman", he finally finished his Master's in Business, has just purchased a new home on the out skirts of Dallas, his mother is doing fine, he'd purchased this Jag for his birthday, this past June.

I listened to him talk. I really didn't want to tell him about me and all of the problems I was having. He didn't say anything on a personal note. He didn't say that he loved me, he didn't say that he missed me, nothing like that. I know, because I was desparately tuning in and hanging onto his every word just to hear him say something to that effect. To keep from looking or sounding foolish, I just listened to him.

Finally, he turned into a new subdivision. The homes in this area were esquisite! The yards were huge! You could tell that it was a work in progress. There were only a few houses that were complete. Kenneth pulled his car into a driveway.

"I want you to see this one," he said. "My company has invested in this project and I was sent here to check on the progress," he continued.

He came to my side of the car, opened the door and helped me out. It's not that women can't do this for themselves, it's not that we want to be pictured as weak and incapable, it's just the principle of the thing. You know, the gentleman's quality, if you will.

I entered into this mansion of a house as Kenneth held the door open for me. I stepped into my dream house! First, my feet stepped onto the off white ceramic tile in the door way and into the foyer. There was a small closet on the left for guest to hang their coats. I could see the huge stair case in front of me. At the base of the stairs was a half bath which contained the bare essentials. It was decorated in deep rich colors; navy, burgundy, green and gold embellishment.

I wanted to rush up stairs! But Kenneth had other plans. He showed me through the arch way on the right. I stepped onto a deep green, plush carpet.

"This is the formal living room," he explained. There was a huge fireplace in the front corner, with a raised hearth. The deep green carpet was warmly inviting. The walls were painted a light taupe color, and the trim was a bright white.

He showed me the dining room which was across from the foyer. There was a built-in hutch on the same wall as the closet in the foyer. The same deep green carpet and paint colors accented this room. From the dining room, he ushered me through a doorway into the kitchen. The emerald green counters were beautiful against the white stained (not painted) cabinets. There was plenty of cabinet space in addition to the cooking island in the center of the kitchen.

From there, we went to the breakfast nook, and on to the den which was to the right of the kitchen and somewhat behind the living room. The den was huge! It also had a fireplace in the corner with a raised hearth. To the rear of the den was a set of double glass doors leading out into an enclosed patio. There was also a second, informally styled stair case in the den that led to the upstairs area. On the other side of the den was a study and a small restroom.

The upstairs opened up into another den! There was a wall covered with cabintry. The cabinets were roomy enough for a big screened TV, stereo system, books, videos, and CD's. The double glass doors opened to a balcony which was over the downstairs patio.

We walked through the six bedrooms! Yes, six! There were six bedrooms and three bathrooms, with one of them being in the master bedroom.

I loved the master bath! The deep green, marbled garden tub, the bubbled glass window, the double sinks, the makeup mirror and lighting, the large shower with it's built in seat and the double enclosed toilets! What more could a girl want?

We finished our tour with Kenneth showing me the three car garage with its open game room on top, the laundry room which was large enough for two dryers, washer, and deep freezer, in addition to the built in cabinets and sink.

We returned to the living room. Kenneth had me to wait there. A few minutes later, he emerged with the picnic basket, the blanket, and a bottle of what looked like champagne. I smiled. He spread the blanket out and prepared the picnic.

The next moments were heavenly. We shared fresh fruit and fruit dip, taking turns feeding each other. There were some fancy cheeses and crackers, and some pastries. It was light, refreshing, and filling. The champagne turned out to be a bubbly, carbonated fruit juice bottled to look like champagne. I didn't mind. I have never been one to indulge in alcoholic beverages anyway.

"Do you like this house?" he asked me.

"Yes, I do!" I replied with excitement in my voice. "Why do you ask?"

"The house I just bought in Dallas is just like this one, right down to the carpet," he said.

"Hmm, very interesting!" I thought, "Very interesting indeed".

We continued making small talk about the house and about how we would decorate it. The time passed by too quickly. Suddenly, there was silence. I realized Kenneth had stopped talking. I looked up to see him staring at me.

"You are so beautiful," he said, almost too softly for me to hear. He leaned towards me. I held my breath. I felt his lips connect with mine. There was that tingling feeling again! While we were kissing, I felt a tear roll down my cheek. God! I love this man! I wiped the tear away before Kenneth could see.

As if he could hear me talking to myself, Kenneth responded by pulling me closer to him and kissing me all the more. I didn't want this moment to end! I reached up and put my arms around his neck. He smelled so good! Every part of my body wanted to scream! Don't stop!

He laid me down onto the floor, still kissing me. I caressed his face with my hand, and then tried to slip my hand into his shirt. I wanted to feel his warm body underneath my hands. I guess he could feel where my mind was headed. He gently grabbed my hand in his and turned in such a way that he began kissing my hand and wrist. I heard him let out a deep sigh. He looked into my eyes.

"Make love to me, you fool!" I wanted to scream!

"I would make love to you, right here and now," he started, as if he could read my thoughts, "but, if I did that, I would have to marry you," he paused, with a sort of chuckle in his voice. "The woman I make love to will be the woman I marry. I have been patiently waiting and praying for the woman who will be my wife." He continued to look into my eyes, as if he was searching for a response, searching for confirmation, searching for something. He leaned onto my body and kissed me again. At that, he smiled and said, "I think we had better stop before we do something we might regret. I just want everything to be right".

He stood up. "I'll be right back," he said. He left the living room and went outside. I jumped up and down—like a two year old having a temper tantrum in a toy store. I wanted to strip down to nothing and be waiting for him when he came back in. For some reason, I knew this would not be a wise thing to do. So instead, I began cleaning up the picnic.

Just as I was finishing up, Kenneth came back into the living room. He stopped for a moment and put whatever it was in his hand into his pocket. He had this puzzled look on his face. He explained he had to get some "fresh air". I tried not to think about that statement too much. He helped me finish cleaning up the picnic.

The ride back to my car was almost in silence. There was so much I felt, that needed to be said. Neither of us could

128

say it. "I love you, Kenneth," I was yelling in my mind. I would look at him and he would look forward. He would look at me and I would look forward. He drove me back to my car which I'd left at the prison unit where I worked. We kissed one last time and said our good-byes.

"I hope to see you again, soon," I told him. I kissed him again. He hugged me like he didn't want to let go. I didn't want to let him go either.

"Well, I've got to head back to Dallas tonight," he said. "This was the best picnic I have ever been on. I hope we can do it again."

He opened my car door for me and helped me in. As I was leaving the parking lot I looked into my rear view mirror. He was still standing next to his car, with the door open, watching me leave.

Chapter 21

MONEY ISN'T EVERYTHING

*A*s I was riding to my house, my mind relived every moment. I wanted to give my body to Kenneth, right then and there. I know it is best to wait. It's so very hard, sometimes.

I turned the corner and headed down my street. I could see that there was a police vehicle in front of my house, with its lights on. I could also see Remo's truck parked in my driveway.

I accelerated my car. My mind started racing. I knew Prince didn't like Remo at all! I was praying that the two of them did not get into any fights. Prince is much smaller and a whole lot less violent than Remo. Remo would take Prince apart.

As I got closer, I could see that Prince's car was not there. That was a relief. "So what's going on?" I wondered.

I walked into my house and saw Officer Mitchell, you know, Cedric, standing there in the living room, taking Remo's statement.

"The stereo, the VCR, the TV, did you get the microwave?" Remo was making a list.

Stereo, TV? I looked around. Oh, my God! My heart sank. Not because of the stuff that was stolen, but I knew somehow, Remo was going to blame me for everything. I knew that he would make this out to be my fault! I turned, back and looked at Cedric in horror.

"It's going to be all right, Angela," he tried to reassure me, patting the air with his hand, to signify somehow, a reassuring pat on my back. He just didn't understand. Remo was going to kill me! I only meant that in the metaphorical sense, even though his attitude and tone indicated otherwise. So far, I was glad to state, he has never put his hands on me to hurt me.

I knew he was going to be so angry because he was the one who had bought all of that stuff for me! I didn't ask him to nor did I need him to. He was always taking it upon himself to buy what he thought I needed or wanted. He was like the Sugar Daddy from the Nightmare on Elm Street! He could buy whatever I wanted, but there was a price! He wanted to rule and run my life!

I quickly ran to my bedroom. Amazingly, nothing in my room had been touched. I went back to Prince's part of the house and saw that his room had not been touched. It almost seemed to me that someone deliberately broke into my house and only took what they knew belonged to or was bought by Remo.

I examined the front door. It was splintered around the door frame where the lock goes into the door jam. Someone did make a forced entry into my house. I doubt that it was Remo.

As violent as he is, he has never tried to come into my house uninvited.

"Angela," Cedric called, "do you see anything else missing?"

"No, I don't think so," I replied.

"Well, you know how to reach me. Either you or Remo call me if you think of something else, or if you come up with some information that can help on this case."

"Okay," I said, nervously. I really wanted to tell Cedric not to leave.

Cedric turned towards Remo and instructed, "Remo, you need to get some things to fix this door for Angela. Can you do that?"

"Yeah, nigga', I know how to take care of my lady," Remo responded with a nasty attitude as he leaned into Cedric's personal space. Remo and Cedric were about the same size, with Remo being about four inches taller the Cedric. However, Cedric was solid muscle and Remo was just, you know, big and thick.

I could tell that Cedric was not happy at all with Remo's statement. He had gotten this look on his face which indicted he was a bit concerned for me and displeased with Remo. He was shaking his note pad in his hand up and down, to go along with the face he was displaying. He turned back towards me. I still had my chin in my hands, sitting on the sofa which was also purchased by Remo.

"You gonna be all right, Angela?" Cedric asked. I could sense his concern.

"I'll be all right. I'll call you in the morning," I promised. With that being said and with Remo on his way out the door to get the supplies to fix the door, Cedric felt confident enough to leave. Before he left completely, though, he stopped by the door, with his hand on the door frame. He turned back and looked at me over his shoulder.

"Has Remo ever hit you?" he asked out of concern.

"No, he never has," I answered honestly. "But he might hit me when he comes back!" I shouted to myself.

"Remember, Angela, I'm just a phone call away."

"Thanks, Ced."

He pulled the door closed as best he could. "Get something and prop it against this door until Remo comes back," he yelled at me through the door.

I got a chair from the small dining room and secured it against the door, underneath the door knob. I mentally began to prepare myself for the verbal debate that was sure to ensue as soon as Remo returned to complete the work on the door.

That was one thing that I could depend on him for. When it came to my safety, he would make sure I was safe. When it was flooding in this area, he gave his truck to me, telling me it was safer and higher off the ground than my car. He drove my car while I had his truck. When I had a flat, on my way from work, I called him. He couldn't come so he sent someone to come and fix the flat. He had already paid the repairmen before sending him to me.

He has his good points, as few as they are. But, he's just not the man for me. He screams, yells, and hollers just too much for me. Although he would buy me the moon if I asked him to, I have learned that money isn't everything!

I busied myself by cleaning up the debre that was strown around the livingroom, while I was waiting for Remo to return. "I wish Kenneth was here," I said out loud, "He wouldn't fix the door. He would just take me to live in one of those six bedrooms in his house. I would even promise to stay in my own room....NOT!" I said, joking to myself.

I heard Remo's truck in the driveway. I removed the chair and went to my bedroom because I didn't want to be around when he completed the repairs on the door.

While I was in my room, I could hear Remo working on the door. The phone rang. It was Patrice.

"I heard what happened!" she started.

"Who told you?" I asked.

"Cedric came by the barber shop and was talking about it. He told Prince to get home as soon as he could."

"I appreciate you letting me know. I was going to call him in a little bit any."

"Are you all right? What's Remo doing? Is he mad?" Patrice, Marilyn and Bam were all familiar with Remo's temper. They know how he can get sometimes.

They were also familiar with my feelings for Kenneth. Most of my fantasies about him, however, and rendezvous with him, I kept secret. I didn't want Remo to find out. The less they knew, the less they would talk. Sometimes, girls just talk too much.

I changed my clothes and put on something I could exercise in, and a pair of tennis shoe. I turned on my small stereo which was still in my room, grabbed my jump rope and began jumping to the rhythm of the music.

I heard Remo's foot steps coming down the hall. I mentally prepared myself. I stopped jumping, turned off the stereo, and put the jump rope on my bed.

"Where in the hell were you?" he started, raising his voice.

"I was at work, Remo"

"I called you on your job first, you weren't there! I know you get off everyday at 3:00, so where in hell have you been since then?"

His voice was getting louder and I could tell he was loosing what little patience he had.

"I had some personal business to take care of when I got off work, if that's any of your business."

"For over four hours?"

He was really angry now. He was stepping closer to me. Sweat was glistening on his body from the work he'd done on the door and with the anger flaring.

"I couldn't get you on your job, so I came by here at about 7 o'clock to take you out to eat. Your door was wide open and all of my stuff was gone." He said, pointing angrily back towards the front door and then towards the empty spaces left by the disappearance of his "stuff".

"You know what?" I felt myself being brave and testing my fate. "I didn't want any of your stuff!" I stood up and got right in his face. "As a matter of fact, I never wanted any of your stuff!" At that, I grabbed the two gold chains that were around my neck that Remo had given to me. I jerked them off my neck and threw them towards my bedroom door.

"Now get your stuff and get out of my house!" It was my turn to point towards the door.

He grabbed me by my arms, near my shoulders and began shaking me violently.

"Girl, I give you whatever you need! Everything you own, just about, came from me! Your clothes, your shoes, this furniture, the refrigerator, EVERYTHING!" he shouted in my face, and then pushed me back onto the bed.

He turned to walk out, huffing and puffing. Why didn't I just let it go? I got up and began grabbing all of the clothes in my closet that were purchased by him; leather coats, suits that still had tags on them, a full length fur coat that I absolutely hated, and shoes!

"Here, take your stuff! Take all of this! I never asked you for it, I don't want it, and all it is doing is taking up space in my closet. And for your information, money isn't everything!"

I was throwing the clothes at him. He stopped and turned back towards me. Fueled with fury, I had emptied about half my closet by the time he turned around. He pressed his way through the barrage of clothes until he was close enough to grab me again. He grabbed me by my shoulders then raised his strong right hand up over his left shoulder as if he was preparing to give me a back handed slap across my face. I shielded my face from his hand. He stopped in mid-motion. Seconds seem like minutes.

Instead of slapping me, he grabbed me by my shoulders again, pulling me to him, pulling my face to his face. His hot breath mixed with the sweat that was now pouring from his face, hit me like a ton of bricks.

He made this growling noise deep in the back of his throat. That look in his eyes said he wanted to kill me. But instead, he pushed me back down on the bed and turned to walk away. Why didn't I just let him go?

This time, when he pushed me back on the bed, my right had landed on the handles of the jump rope I'd been using. I grabbed it, lunged towards him, making my own growling sound and commenced to beat him across his back with that rope! I was so angry!

I hit him maybe two times, before he turned around and took a hold of the rope. It didn't even seem to faze him. With my third swing, he turned and put up his arm. He was able to grab the rope when it hit him and he wrapped the rope around his arm then jerked it from my hands.

"Okay, now what do you do?" I asked myself, "You can't run because he's blocking the door, and to be honest, you hit him first!"

I couldn't move as he walked towards me again. By this time, his eyes were bloodshot and he was still sweating. My heart was racing! I had to fight to keep the tears from my eyes. I stood there, unmoving, with my arms folded across my chest. I stood there, not wanting to reveal the fear that was quickly taking over my mind and body. He reached up and grabbed my face with one hand, and shook the rope in my face with the other.

"I'm tired of playing these games, little girl. Now clean up this mess," he said, pointing around my room in a circular motion. I hated when he called me "little girl".

This time, he didn't push me back onto the bed. He threw the rope into the corner of my bedroom. He turned to leave, picking up both gold chains and putting them in his pocket. I heard the door slam. I heard his truck leave.

I fell to the floor and just let go of a cry that I felt I deserved and my courage could no longer contain. I started picking up the clothes, folding some of them and putting them on my bed, and hanging some of the others.

At some point, I must have fallen asleep. Prince came home and found me lying on the floor, amongst the rest of the clothes I had pulled from my closet. He kneeled down to pick me up. At first it startled me, and then I realized it was him; a welcomed sight. I reached up to hug him, he hugged me back.

"What happened?" he wanted to know.

I shared the whole story with him, right down to the jump rope part. Prince was one I could tell everything and he wouldn't tell anyone.

Chapter 22

THINGS GO FROM BAD TO WORSE

*T*he next morning, I really wanted to call in sick for work. I was just too tired, too emotionally drained, achey, and there were two bruises now visible on my arms. I just couldn't pull myself together enough to make it to work. In spite of the way I was feeling, I dragged myself out of bed and started getting dressed.

I was really feeling sorry for myself. On the one hand I have this man that would do anything for me, so it seemed; then, on the other hand, there is this man that invades my dreams, my thoughts, and my visions of the future. He seems to be everything I have hoped for and prayed for, for so long. Why, then, does it seem as if we'll never be together? My head was throbbing, thinking about the messed up state of my love life.

"Maybe I'll just die a virgin," I pitied myself. "Who would want me anyway? I'm just a 'plain Jane'," I yelled out loud, throwing my hands in defeat. I was really taking this opportunity to have a pity party.

I really wanted to cry, but I knew if I went to work, I would be forced not to cry because the offenders would ask too many questions. I reasoned with myself and agreed that going to work would be in my best interest. Besides, today is Friday and Fridays are always easy days.

As I continued getting dressed and completed my self analysis, I had to come to grips with something. I realized that the reason Remo and I can't get along is because we are too much alike. We are both sensitive and we both want to be loved so much. But, we both have these mean streaks. Where Kenneth's love and tenderness soothes the ugly nature that I am capable of, Remo just seems to add fuel to my fire. He wants his way all of the time. And, because I refuse to surrender my will and my world to him, the negative sides of us both just explode with the potential power and devastation of a volcanic eruption. I was beginning to believe that in some way, I intimidated him. I know that I frustrated him because I wouldn't just let him do and be for me everything he wanted to do and be.

I thought back over our relationship. I realized how much was wasted over the last three years. Not only have I wasted my time with Remo, but I have wasted my emotions. I have also wasted my energy, my support, my fears, my hopes, my dreams and my future. I realized that I cannot afford to waste anything else on this relationship with Remo.

I won't go so far as to say that I didn't deserve Remo, but I would say that he didn't deserve *me*. He needed someone who would love and appreciate all of the fine things he could offer. He needed someone he could protect, someone he could lead and make decisions for. He needed someone who would love to be cared for, but at the same time, someone he would not be afraid to *love*. He needed someone who needed everything that he has to offer. I don't hate Remo, but I know I don't love him. I am just not the one for him. I finished getting dressed and made my way to work.

My class started out as usual. I passed out my sign in sheet and began handing out the assignments for the day. As the offenders began their task, I took my seat at my desk. I had an uneasy feeling in the pit of my stomach, so I looked up and began to visually examine each student in my class.

Thomas was sitting in his normal seat, obviously upset about something. His face was red and swollen from crying, and he was not doing any work. He was just sitting there.

"Is something wrong Thomas?" I asked. There was no response from him. "Thomas, is there something you want to talk about today?" I asked again. If something was really wrong, or if he was going to be trouble for me and my other students, I needed to get him out of my class room as quickly as possible.

"I just don't understand, Ms. West." He said, with a voice that indicated he was troubled.

"You don't understand what, Thomas?"

"Why I'm here, that's what I don't understand." His agitation was increasing.

"Thomas, now I don't understand."

"I'm just a little thief," he explained. "I stole some stuff and I got caught so I have to come to jail, but now their telling me that I got some charges for messing with kids and I might get a whole lot more time! I don't understand!"

"Thomas, what are you talking about?"

"It's right here in black and white," Thomas shouted, shaking some papers that he had sitting on his desk. "All I wanted to do was go home to my daddy's funeral and when I put in for a furlough they told me I can't 'cause I got these charges against me that are still out there!"

I had Thomas pass the papers up to me so that I could read them and maybe explain to him what was going on. I tried to keep the other students calm, telling them to get back to their assignments. I quickly read through Thomas' papers and he was right! Not only was there a formal notice from his home town indicating his father died, but there was also the denial of his furlough and a warrant for his arrest, issued by the state of Louisiana for some unresolved child molestation charges.

"I need to go home!" Thomas shouted and beat his fist on his desk.

"Thomas, you are..."

"I said I want to go home!" he shouted even louder and beat his fist on the desk again. The other students had stopped working. I knew I would have to get the situation under control before something bad happened.

"Okay, Thomas. I'm going to call and see about getting you out of here so you will be able to go to your father's funeral," I lied. Instead, I picked up the phone and called the security desk that was in the education department for emergencies such as this one. Officer Gray answered the phone.

"Security desk, Officer Gray, can I help you?" she asked. Officer Gray is one of those officers who takes her job seriously. Even though she is a female, she has a stocky frame and can hold her own when it comes to handling these offenders.

"Yes," I responded. "I have this offender here who needs to go home to his father's funeral." I was desperately trying to provide a hint that I needed some assistance.

"You need some help, Ms. West?" she asked.

"Yes, I do." I responded.

"Is one of them fools acting up?" she asked with a slight smirk. I really think she likes her job.

"Yes ma'am. And if you could provide me with the proper assistance, I would greatly appreciate it."

"Yes, ma'am, I'll be right there."

141

While I was talking to Officer Gray on the phone, I used my free hand to access information on my computer about Thomas and I kept my eyes on him. I pulled up his medical screen and saw the notation which indicated Thomas has a history of mental illness.

"Where's he at, Ms. West?" Officer Gray asked as she entered the class room. She looked around the room and before I could answer her, she had already identified Thomas by his red face. She went and stood by his desk.

"Is this him?" she asked, pointing down at him. Thomas just sat there, with his hands in his lap, underneath the desk top, and he kept his head down.

"What's the matter with you, boy?" Officer Gray had her left hand on the desk top and her right hand on the back part of the seat. She was leaning over, trying to make eye contact with Thomas. Thomas just kept his head down.

"You in the penitentiary now, man. You ain't goin' nowhere! You did the crime, so do the time! Quit crying! Suck it up, player!" Ms. Gray was firm to all of the offenders she came in contact with. However, in this incident, I don't think her firmness was appreciated. After she made her comments to Thomas, she straightened up and provided me with her report.

"He's gonna be alright, Ms. West. Just call me if you have any more problems," she smiled, feeling as if her counseling session was a success.

But, before she could move away from Thomas' desk, he reached into the waist band of his pant, pulled out an object, jumped up from his seat and grabbed Ms. Gray around her neck! Everything happened too quickly for her to respond. With a firm grip on Officer Gray's neck and the object pointed at her throat, Thomas began making his way towards the rear of the classroom, to prevent anyone from sneaking up behind him. Since my desk is near the door, there was really no other place for Thomas to go.

The other offenders knew the drill. They immediately abandoned their desk and parted like the Red Sea, making their way to the opposite sides of the classroom. They knew that they were supposed to get down on the floor. This would help other officers who responded to the situation, to know who was involved in the incident and who was not.

"I said I want to go home!" Thomas demanded.

"Thomas, I want to help you to get home, but you've got to help me." I tried to calm him down.

"You lied!" he shouted, pointing his now visible metal homemade knife at me. He maintained his tight grip around Officer Gray's neck. "You said you were gonna help me, but you lied!" I could see and hear Thomas' desperation increasing as the moments ticked by. This situation is the epitome of my life. Both of them were going from bad to worse.

I came from behind my desk, amazingly calm, trying to sooth Thomas. It was my training that kicked in. It was not that I felt strong; it was not that I felt I could out maneuver this offender; it was not even as though I felt that Thomas was going to give up on my command. No, the only thing that kept me from loosing control all together is the training that I received when I first started teaching for the prison system.

"Come on, Thomas. Let me get you some real help. I'm sure these things can be worked out," I said as softly as I could. I didn't want to upset him any more than he was. I continued easing my way towards him as he continued holding Officer Gray.

"Stay right there!" He suddenly shouted, pointed the knife in my direction again. "Stay right there before I have to hurt somebody!" He was saying through his tears and desperation. "I don't want to hurt nobody!" He really stared crying and jabbing the small knife into his leg. Soon I could see blood stains on his white uniform, where he stabbed himself. I realized I had to do something. The back up staff was just taking too long.

"Thomas, why don't you and I just sit here and talk about all of this," I said, tapping on one of the desk close to me.

I looked into Officer Gray's eyes to make sure she was alright. When I did, I saw that she was motioning with her eyes and her thumb, in a hitchhiking fashion, trying to get me to move to Thomas' right side. I moved slowly into the direction her eyes were moving. I kept my focus on Thomas and then on her. All the while I was moving, taking small steps, I kept up my conversation with Thomas, trying to keep him as calm as I could. His right arm, the one holding the knife was still pointing at me, following me, as Thomas was talking.

Thomas failed to realize that as I was moving and he was following me, his hold and stance on Officer Gray widened. That must have been what she was anticipating. As soon as Thomas' stance and grip were open enough and he was distracted enough, Officer Gray turned into the grip, facing Thomas, and at the same time, she hit him in the face with an upper elbow thrust.

The unexpected strike caused Thomas to stumble. That gave Officer Gray the opportunity that she needed. She followed her first elbow strike with a knee to the groin. When Thomas went down, she struck him in the back of his neck, at a pressure point, causing Thomas to collapse to the floor.

About that time, reinforcements entered the room. The other offenders remained seated on the floor as they began to cheer Officer Gray for saving all of us.

It took a while, but my class was able to settle down so that we could make the best of the rest of our class time. I was almost too nervous to continue. Every time there was a sudden sound or a sudden move, I would jump. Before leaving work, I promised myself to speak with my principal about a thirty day leave of absence. I could not take the drama any longer.

Chapter 23

SEEKING GOOD ADVICE

*T*he day lasted a little longer than I wanted it to. There were so many reports I had to complete regarding the incident with Thomas. Officer Gray managed to go on with her duties. She has had incidents like this before. Not quite as life threatening, but just as dangerous as this. She is a professional and she enjoys her work. For me, I was more ready to leave the unit today, than I have ever been.

As I was leaving the unit, I clutched my approval for a thirty day leave in my hand. As I was walking out of the unit, I glanced at it several times, reassuring myself that the approval had been signed. My principal completely understood why I wanted and needed to be off. I promised him that I would keep in touch and let him know if I needed more than thirty days.

I didn't go straight home. I just needed some time to think and reflect. I went to one of those salad bar restaurants and ate alone. My thoughts vacillated between all of the things that have transpired over the course of the past few weeks. My thoughts went from Kenneth, to Remo, to the burglary, to Remo and back to Kenneth. I needed someone to talk to.

I finished my meal and was making my way home when I decided to detour and go by Ms. Dee's. I knew it was late and that she would probably be gone, but I just needed to talk to someone I trusted.

I was so glad to find Ms. Dee's white truck in the parking lot and the lights still on in the shop when I arrived. I knocked on the door trying to get Ms. Dee's attention. She came around the corner and smiled when she saw me.

"Come on in, Angela, I knew somebody would be coming by here tonight to see me. What can I do for you?" Ms. Dee had that ability. She had that right relationship with God. She heard His voice and she was always obedient when He gave her instructions. I'm glad the Lord told her to wait for me tonight.

"Hi, Ms. Dee, I just needed to talk to someone. I have been going through a lot lately," I talked as she locked the door and ushered me to the back and we made our way to the break room. We both sat down and she listened attentively while I spoke. I told her the truth about how I felt about Remo, Kenneth, and the incident that happened on the unit today. I didn't tell her about all of the violence between Remo and me. Some things are just too shameful to talk about. I surprised myself by the fact that I was able to share my story with her, without crying. Ms. Dee just listened.

"Have you prayed about any of this?" she asked after a few moments of silence.

"Yes, Ms. Dee, I have," I half confessed.

"What does the Lord say about it all?" Ms. Dee would always start by asking those two questions. I guess it was her test to measure the faith of the person she was talking too.

"I don't hear Him the way you do, Ms. Dee," I replied.

"That's because you don't trust Him like I do. I hear Him because I expect to hear Him when I talk to Him and ask Him for something."

Ms. Dee was right. Although I pray, I feel that I have done so much wrong that God wouldn't hear me and if he heard me He wouldn't waste His time answering my prayer.

"The next time you pray, start out by repenting of those things you know are not right. Then ask Him to bless you with His will in your life and ask Him to open up whatever it is He has for you and block and remove those things that are not for you."

I nodded my head in agreement with Ms. Dee. She always provided good advice, but she makes you do the work to receive your own blessing from God. She wouldn't just pray *for* you, but she would pray with you or teach you to pray and tell you to go pray yourself.

While we were talking, we suddenly heard noises in the alley behind the shop. We both stopped talking and looked towards the emergency exit that was located at the rear of the building, in the break room where we were talking. As we looked at each other, I was wondering what to do, but Ms. Dee stood up. She knew what to do. She took quick steps to the storage room and emerged with a baseball bat. She started walking back to the emergency exit.

"What are you doing, Ms. Dee?" I asked nervously.

"I'm going to see what's going on in my alley!" she said matter-of-factly. There was not too much that frightened Ms. Dee. She would always say that she is "covered by the blood".

"You can't go back there by yourself!" I shouted, exposing my own fears. She may have been covered by the blood but I was not sure if I was.

"Well, come on, then," she said, motioning to me with the bat to follow her.

I got real close behind Ms. Dee. I felt it was better for her to go first. She's got that voice of authority, rebuking things in the name of Jesus, cross carrying, devil you're defeated kind of faith. I was just glad that she didn't have a problem with being first.

The alley was dimly lit. We could see a small vehicle parked a few feet from where we were standing. The car was rocking back and forth, obviously from the movement of the people inside. We couldn't see any heads in the car so we both figured that whoever it was, they were lying on the floor of the car.

"Who's in there?" Ms. Dee yelled, but she did not make any additional steps closer to the car. She still had the bat raised in her hands, ready to strike if the situation called for it.

There was no response from the car so Ms. Dee took a few steps closer to the car. I came up behind her after I was sure that no mass murderer was going to jump out of the car and attack us.

"Who's in there?" Ms. Dee yelled again, this time tapping the bat on the trunk of the car. After Ms. Dee tapped on the trunk of the car, the rocking stopped and a head popped up from the back seat. We were now close enough to see that it was Grady's old blue Toyota. He'd been by Ms. Dee's earlier during the day, to drop off supplies.

"Grady!" Ms. Dee yelled with a shrill in her voice which depicted her anger. "Shady Grady, come on out of that car, right now!" Ms. Dee was really angry. I was trying hard not to laugh. I could only imagine who it was that Grady had in the car with him.

"Grady! Herman Grady!" Now I know Ms. Dee was angry. Nobody calls him "Herman". Ms. Dee went back to the emergency door and grabbed the water hose that was hanging there. She turned the water on full blast and headed back to Grady's car. I just moved out of the way.

"Grady! Come out of that car right now! You and whoever you have in there with you, come out!" At that, Ms. Dee opened the back door and began showering the inhabitants of the car with the spray from the water hose.

Shady Grady finally emerged, soaking wet, from the car. Fortunately, for us, he still had his clothes on. He had lip stick kisses all over his head, face and neck. Behind him, Ya'Shika slowly emerged from the car. She was buttoning her blouse, but still had the rest of her clothes on.

I had to work hard at not laughing at them as an unlikely couple. Ya'Shika stands head and shoulders taller than Grady. She looked as if she could swallow him whole. She was standing there with her arm wrapped around Grady's neck and her hand resting on top of his head. As Ya'Shika smiled to camouflage her shame, her pink tongue was visible through the gap in her front teeth.

"You two ought to be ashamed of yourselves!" Ms. Dee instructed me to turn off the water.

"Grady, you are a grown man. You are too old to be playing these foolish games. And you, Ya'Shika, should know by now that if a man only wants to sleep with you, and does not even have the decency to offer you a room, he is not worth sleeping with!" She was preaching at both of them, with one hand on her hip and furiously pointing her finger at them, with her other hand. They both just stood there, listening to every word.

"Do you love her?" Ms. Dee asked Grady.

"Well, uh, I don't know, Ms. Dee," Grady responded.

"Before you sleep with her again, you should know whether or not you love her. You understand me?" Ms. Dee instructed and chastised all at the same time. Grady just nodded and hung his head down. I don't know what made him more ashamed; the fact that he was caught or the fact that he was caught with Ya'Shika.

"Ya'Shika, you need to examine yourself. Quit giving your body away like it's a dirty rag at a car wash! If you would quit allowing men to use you, then they wouldn't use you! Have more pride than what you are displaying to me right now, young lady." Ms. Dee was being very stern to the both of them.

"Now, what I want the two of you to do is; you, Grady, take Ya'Shika home so that she can shower and put on some decent clothes. You go get showered and dressed, then you take her out to dinner and treat her like a lady. If you treat her like a lady she will act like one."

They both nodded their heads in agreement, entered the front seats of the car, and left. Ms. Dee was satisfied, believing she made a difference in two lives. She confessed to me that she's known for a long time that Toya, Ya'Shika's youngest daughter, is Grady's child.

I helped Ms. Dee lock up the shop and headed home. I felt rejuvenated and refreshed. I felt revived by the talk that Ms. Dee and I had, as well as encouraged by the potential romance blossoming between Grady and Ya'Shika. If Ya'Shika could get her man, I could get mine!

Chapter 24

AND THE TRUTH....

*A*s I drove home, I felt a degree of relief. With my thirty day leave, I would have plenty of time to think things through. I would have time to think through my relationship with Remo, my relationship with Kenneth, and my job. My job was the most pressing issue on my mind at that moment. With the attack on Ms. Gray still fresh in my mind, I had to decide if I was going to go back or teach in the public school system.

I went into the house, glad to be home. As I walked past the coffee table in the living room, I saw a black box with a small white ribbon around it. At closer examination, I saw that the box was for me.

The box contained the two gold chains that I had ripped from my neck during an earlier escapade with Remo. There was also a new gold chain. Although I was impressed that Remo had the chains repaired and impressed by the new chain, I could not help but wonder how he got the box in my house. I was sure the door was locked. I thought back before I entered for the evening and distinctly remembered I had to unlock the door before coming in.

There was also a new stereo system set up on my stand, a TV, VCR, and a microwave oven was sitting on the floor, near the kitchen door, still in the box. There was not doubt in my mind that Remo bought these things, replacing what was stolen.

"Maybe Prince let him in," I reassured myself. I put all three chains back into the box and left the box on the coffee table. I made a mental note to give them and the rest of the items back to Remo. The first thing I needed to do to end this relationship with Remo is to stop taking gifts from him. I was proud of myself for taking a firm stand.

I was on my way to my bed room when the phone rang. I ran to it, hoping it was Kenneth.

"Hello?" I asked nervously.

"Angela?" It was Patrice. It was obvious that she was upset and in some dramatic situation again.

"Yes, Patrice. What is it? Calm down!"

"I am so sorry!"

"Sorry? Sorry for what?"

"It was Derrick who broke into your house!"

"I kind of figured that. But, why are you calling? What's wrong?"

"I'm calling because I'm in jail! I was arrested!"

"Patrice!" Now, I was getting excited. "What do you mean, 'arrested'?"

"The cops came by my apartment and asked to look around. I told them they could because they didn't tell me what they were looking for or anything. They looked in the little shed on my patio and found all of your stuff! I am so sorry!"

"Patrice, you have nothing to be sorry about! What I don't understand is why they arrested you? Where's Derrick? Why didn't he get arrested?"

"He was arrested yesterday for having some cocaine on him. He told the cops that he could tell them about a burglary,

152

if they would let him go. He told them about your house being robbed and said that I did it!"

"You know what, Patrice, I believe every word you just said. We have been telling you that Derrick is no good. Now that you have seen the truth about him, maybe you can let him go."

"I am so ready to be rid of him! I know Derrick is not perfect and I know he has his problems, but this is something I never would have expected, even from him."

"Well, I'm going to call Bam and we will be there in a few minutes to get you out. I'm going to make sure Derrick gets the blame for this one.

"Okay. Thank you, Angela. I am so, so sorry!" Patrice was still crying when we ended our phone call.

I called Bam and explained the situation to her. She was just as angry as I was that Derrick would sacrifice Patrice to save his own neck. Bam was ready to execute Derrick by the time I finished telling her of Patrice's situation.

We ended our conversation and agreed to meet at the police station. I left a note for Prince, telling him that Patrice had been arrested and that I'd gone to the police station to get her out.

By the time I arrived, Bam had already made it there. She was in the process of signing some papers to get Patrice released. She also presented me with papers that formally charged Derrick with the burglary. I allowed the property to remain in custody so that forensics could conduct their investigation. We were all positive that fingerprints would turn out to be Derrick's and possibly Derrick's alone. At any rate, we were definitely sure that Patrice's fingerprints were not on any of my property.

With that matter being settled, Patrice was able to get away from Bam without a long negative discussion about Derrick. I think even Bam realized that Patrice had seen the light as far as Derrick is concerned. There was no need to dwell on the subject, considering all of the emotional strain Patrice had just endured with being arrested and falsely accused.

I took Patrice to get a bite to eat. She explained that she had not eaten since lunch time. I paid for her meal, knowing that she did not have any money. When she was arrested, she was not allowed to take anything with her, not even the keys to her apartment.

After getting her food, I drove her home to her place. We rode in silence. She ate the food, hardly looking up from the bag.

When we arrived at her apartment, I was not surprised to find the door wide open. The lights were off. I decided to go up with her just to make sure everything was alright. Once inside, we knew who'd been there. Her purse was on the kitchen counter, open, with the contents spread out. Patrice examined her purse and quickly discovered that the few dollars she had in her purse were gone.

"I can't believe Derrick!" She said. "He took all of the money that I had until my next payday." It was amazing to me how calm she was. I would have been ready to scream.

"Here, Patrice. Take this." I said as I reached into my purse and withdrew $100 in mixed bills. "Do you have anything that needs to be taken care of right now?"

"No. I just need gas money and money to eat on. I'll pay you back when..."

"Don't worry about it, Patrice. Just promise me, you will not let Derrick back into your apartment."

"I promise," she said. We hugged each other. I heard her let out a sigh of relief.

"Make sure you get these locks changed tomorrow!" I yelled at her as I was leaving. She promised again that she would.

On my way home, I saw Remo's truck parked at a local theater. I was compelled to pull into the parking lot. I was curious to see who he was with. I found a parking space a few rows behind his, I parked and turned off my engine and lights and waited. It was not long before I saw him emerge from the theater with someone holding onto his arm. As they got closer to his truck I could clearly see who it was. I was not shocked at all to see Remo coming out of a movie theater with one of his hoochies.

I watched them walk to Remo's truck. They were both looking at each other, talking. The way the young lady was dressed, I was sure that she was trying to seduce Remo. When they arrived at his truck, Remo leaned the young girl against his truck, then leaned his body onto hers and gave her a kiss.

I searched myself, looking for any sign of jealousy, any sign of anger, or any kind of hurt feeling. There was nothing! I did not feel anything! As a matter of fact I laughed! I was so very relieved! I thought it was going to be hard for me to separate myself for him. He just gave me the ammunition that I needed!

I waited until Remo and the young lady left the parking lot in Remo's truck. I didn't want him to know that I saw him.

On my way home, the more and more I thought about the evening, the better I felt! This was a night of truths being revealed! Grady and Ya'Shika may have found their mates in each other. Patrice's eyes have been opened about Derrick, and I am free of Remo!

"And the truth will set you free!" I shouted to myself as I continued driving home.

Chapter 25

FAITH IS IN THE EYE OF THE BELIEVER

*T*he next Sunday morning, I prepared for church. Friday night was such a triumphant day that I decided to give God all the glory and praise. I had a new attitude about so much in my life. I'd even changed my hairstyle and allowed Ms. Dee to give me a fancy hairdo instead of my regular. My thoughts were alive with the new possibilities.

The service was pretty good. Marilyn sang her heart out. She played and sang a song that she'd written. It was all about faith being in the eye of the believer. She sang that faith has nothing to do with what you see, but everything to do with what you have the faith to believe. The song was very moving and it ministered to me.

The pastor preached on faith, using the story of Joseph. He titled his message, *"From the Pit to the Palace"*. He talked about how Joseph never gave up, even after he was sold into slavery. God showed Joseph several times that he would be an important leader. Although nothing seemed to be happening, Joseph kept his faith in God. Even when things went from bad to worse, Joseph kept the faith. Before Joseph died, everything God promised him came to past.

All during the sermon, I kept hearing this "voice" reassuring me that Kenneth was the one that I would marry. I kept fighting back my tears. It was too good to be true! I mean, how would that happen? It had been a little over seven years since I first met him.

"Look how long Joseph had to wait," the voice said, "God is doing a work in you to prepare you to receive the gift He has for you."

"Well, God…what's the hold up? Is it me? C'mon then, fix ME! I'm ready to be fixed!" I shouted to myself in the midst of my tears.

After church, I could hardly contain myself. I thought about the tee shirt I'd purchased from RAG Apparel several weeks earlier. It was still in plain view, on a chair near my bed. I meditated on its caption, thinking about the words, now more empowered with the confirming words of my pastor.

I felt a fresh, new surge of excitement. It was as if I had been lifted out of my own pit and it was now time to take my place in my own success. I was ready for my own promotion to the palace. I have done my time in the pit and I was ready to move on up. It has been a long seven years, but, as my pastor said, "Look how long Joseph had to wait!"

I was reminded of my prayer that I made to God so long ago when I asked God for the man I am to marry. I compared what I asked God for to Kenneth:

He is a gentle man and a gentleman.

He respects me and has never tried anything inappropriate.

He is a Christian.

He is tall and handsome.

I have never heard or seen him angry.

He's romantic.

Even his shadow of a beard has blossomed into a full beard. And, most importantly, the first time I met him, he opened the door for me!

Kenneth must be the one for me! I was excited by the possibility. The rest of the day was filled with thoughts and dreams of finally becoming one with Kenneth. I thought about how easy it would be for me to move to Dallas. I am a teacher, I can teach anywhere in the state. He already has a house! This would be easy for me.

While all of these thoughts were going on in my mind and heart, I made the decision to open up my heart one last time. I wrote another letter to Kenneth. I poured my heart out to him again. This time I didn't change or leave out a thing!

We'd been writing letters to each other over the last seven years. We both agreed that letters are romantic and fun to receive. I chose to write a letter this time because I wanted it to contain everything that I was feeling for Kenneth. My feelings and emotions were so full, there was no way I could call him and speak the words out loud, telling him everything I was feeling. My tears would choke the words right out of my mouth.

I completed my letter and read it through a second time to make sure I did not leave out a thing. I decided that I would immediately take the letter to the post office. I did not want to take the chance of reasoning with myself and convincing myself not to mail the letter. I purchased a stamped envelope from the vending machine at the post office and I immediately put the letter in the mail, before I could loose my courage. Right before I placed the letter into the mail box, I sealed it with a prayer and a kiss.

Chapter 26

IT'S OVER

Coming home from the post office, I approached my house and saw Remo's truck sitting in my drive way. I didn't like the way he was coming over whenever he felt like it.

When I went in, Remo was sitting on the sofa with my keepsake box in front of him, reading my letters from Kenneth. It was obvious he'd been in my house for a while because of all of the letters that were on display. I was livid! Not only was he uninvited, but somehow, he'd gotten into my house and was going through my private things!

"This is my private stuff, Remo," I said, trying to remain calm and picking up the letters and returning them to the box. I was glad to see that my precious dried rose had not been removed from the safety of the waxed paper I had enclosed it in.

"Who in the hell is Kenneth?" he asked, shaking the letter he had in his hand.

"He's just a friend!" I shouted back.

"Looking at these letters, this nigga's more than some friend!" Remo shouted at me, waving the letters he'd been reading in my direction. Remo stood up from the sofa, threw the letters back into the box and grabbed one of the pictures of Kenneth.

"What is this supposed to mean?" He shouted, shoving the picture in my face. I had to back away so that I could see what he was talking about. I grabbed the picture and walked over to the front window, under the pretense of getting a better look.

There on the lower corner of his picture, Kenneth had writtent the words, *"With love, hugs and kisses, Kenneth"*. During the seven years of our friendship, Kenneth and I had shared numerous photos back and forth. At least once a year, I would send him an updated picture of me, and he would send a picture of himself to me. I knew Remo would be angry, so after he came into my life I put all of Kenneth's pictures and sacred letters in my keepsake box.

"That's just something friends write on their pictures," I said as I carried the picture back to the sanctity of my box and closed the lid. Then I picked up the box and carried it to the living room closet, trying to protect the rest of my precious momentos from Remo's wrath.

"What are you doing in my house anyway?" my thoughts shifted. "Who gave you permission to come in my house, go in my room, in my closet and through my personal things?" I felt my voice raising. I was still trying to maintain my composure. I could tell Remo was angry. He was pacing back and forth, with his hands on his hips, breathing heavily, like a wild animal in a cage. Lately, Remo's behavior was becoming more unpredictable and more violent. I started picking up and securing the other letters that were sitting on the living room table.

"How did you get in here any way?" I asked. I really wanted to know how he was able to get into my house. I was expecting him to say that Prince let him in before he left.

Instead, he said, "I've got a key!" He took his key ring out of his pocket and shook the keys to emphasize his statement. I could plainly see my shiny new house key dangling from his chain.

"When I fixed the front door, I kept a set of the keys for myself. As much stuff as I own in this house, I deserve a key."

"You don't live here and I never gave you permission to come into my home whenever you felt like it."

"I own all of this in here!" he yelled, pointing around the room.

"Well, take all this here and get out," I mimicked his pointing all around the room. My sarcasm must have really made him angry, because in one smooth move, he stepped across the coffee table, grabbed me by my arm and pulled me closer to him.

"Who you think you playing with, little girl? Hunh? Who you think you playing with?" I hated it when he said that to me. I hated the way he talked to me. But mostly, I hated to see Remo so angry. Most of the time, he would just get angry, explode and leave. For some reason, with the look in his eyes, I didn't thing he was going to just leave. His eyes were bloodshot, his nose was flared and I could see the veins in his neck. He was also clenching his teeth.

My sarcasm quickly turned to fear as he tightened his grip on my arm.

"Let go of me! You're hurting me!" I tried to maintain my composure as I desperately fought back my tears. I couldn't let him see me go weak.

"Are you sleeping with him?"

"What are you talking about?

"Are you sleeping with him?" As he yelled louder, spit flew in my face.

"No!" I said honestly, "He lives in Dallas." This situation was quickly escalating and I tried to think of a way to get out of it.

"You are the one who is sleeping around!" I shouted back at him.

"What are you talking about?"

"I saw you and your little hoochie leaving the movie theater Friday night!"

"That girl is nothing but a quick piece of...!" He unrighteously defended himself. He knows I hate it when he curses so much so over the years he has tried to cut back. "You are the one I want. She was just a two dollar trick!" he continued.

If I was not so afraid, I would have attacked his statements. The situation reminded me of Sylvester and how he treated me so long ago. Was that what he thought of me? A two dollar trick? Well, it didn't matter now. All that mattered at that moment was that I get out of the situation with Remo so that I could end my fake relationship and get on with my life.

"Just because you are not being faithful to me, it doesn't mean that I'm cheating on you," I defended myself.

"Yes you are!" he accused, "That's why I can't get none from you, 'cause you giving it to him!" He paused, and got closer to my face. "Ain't nobody gonna take what belongs to me," he said firmly, through his clenched teeth.

I knew he was serious. This time, he was going to hurt me. I fought my fear as I started thinking of a way to free myself. I was reaching around in the air until my hand landed on a huge crystal figurine that was on the coffee table. With everything in me, I swung the figurine, trying to hit him in the head. Unfortunately for me, he saw it coming towards him. In his efforts to dodge my swing and my weapon, he stumbled and loosened his grip from my arm.

I managed to break away from him and ran to my bedroom, trying to stay away from him. I couldn't run towards the front door because he was blocking my path. Just as I was proping a chair in front of my bedroom door, Remo kicked the door in on his first attempt. I staggered backwards from the force.

Remo rushed into the room and pushed me down on the bed. He started removing his clothes, pushing me back down, every time I tried to get up and get away from him.

He removed his shirt and started on his pants. While he was bent over, with his pants down by his knees, my eyes were filled with another revealing truth. He was wearing boxers! Not white ones, but boxers! They were navy with yellow anchors. He was desperately trying to get his shoes off. While he was preoccupied, I moved further up onto the bed.

Anger and courage returned to me. I jumped up on the bed and kicked him in the groin. As he fell over onto the bed, I jumped off. But, before I could get to the door, he grabbed my foot, causing me to fall to the floor. He was holding his throbbing groin in one hand and grabbing at me with the other.

I kicked at him with my free foot, trying to get away. But, he was just too strong for me. He managed to restrict my movements and pin me down with his body on top of me. I was struggling and screaming as he was trying to get my clothes off. The growing situation between Remo and me was so intense that we were both unaware that Prince had entered the room with a broken broom handle.

Prince swung the stick and struck Remo across his back. Seemingly unfazed, Remo looked up at Prince, grabbed the stick in the middle of Prince's second swing, pretty much the same way he grabbed the jump rope from me.

Remo started on Prince, landing two punches on his face. Lucky for Prince, Remo was slow and sloppy. After those first two punches, Remo had a difficult time trying to land another punch. Prince managed to dodge Remo's additional swings.

I took the opportunity to dial 911. The response officer assured me that an officer was on the way.

"I've called the police, Remo" I yelled, trying to get his attention. "You'd better leave. And as far as I am concerned, our relationship or whatever you want to call it—it's over! I don't ever want to see you again."

163

Remo could see that I had the phone in my hand and the serious look on my face. He picked up his clothes and left. I was still surprised but relieved that he did give in so quickly and left.

I went over to Prince and hugged him. We checked each other for injuries. I saw blood trickling from a cut on Prince's chin and I could see he had a small cut above his eye. He looked me over and with the exception of the bruises that I had, I was without any injuries.

"Thank you," I told him.

He just looked at me and nodded his head. I could tell he was weary due to the fight with Remo. I was glad he came to my rescue but I had to admit that he really put his life in danger, trying to save me. I didn't want him to put his life on the line for me anymore.

By the time Cedric arrived, Remo had been gone for a while. Cedric took our statements and said he would file the necessary report in order to get charges filed against Remo. He explained that I would have to go to the police station in the morning and sign the formal complaint and get a restraining order.

Cedric left and I took a closer look at Prince's injuries. After patching up the cuts on Prince's chin and over his eye, I took a long hot shower. My body was still shaking and I was feeling quite achy from the stress of this last confrontation with Remo. I had to fight to keep my mind from thinking about what could have happened if Prince had not come when he did.

After my shower, I found Prince sitting on the sofa with his head back and his eyes closed, and his hands shielding his eyes.

"You know, cuz, we can't keep going on like this," he started.

"What do you mean?' I asked.

"Me, you, and Remo," he calmly responded.

"I'm glad you came when you did." I thanked him again for delivering me.

"Yeah, but the next time I might not be here. Then what?" he asked.

"I'm sorry you are in the middle of my troubles."

"Cuz, I love you but you've got to make a decision before one of us ends up dead and another one of us ends up in jail. You don't have to stay here and put up with him. Why can't women see that? There are so many good and gentle guys who would appreciate the opportunity to be with somebody like you and..." his voice trailed off as he let out a deep sigh of exhaustion and relief.

You're right" I agreed with him half heartedly.

Prince's statement hit me like a ton of bricks. Then a light clicked on in my head. I felt relief come over me. "He's right!" I thought to myself. "I don't have to stay here and go through this."

I gave Prince a hug and kiss, checked the door and went to my room.

I picked up my tee-shirt, "Prayer is the Key, but Faith Will Make You Get up Off Your Knees and Work". I gave it a hug, as I was reflecting on my pastor's sermon. My faith was renewed. I kneeled in prayer.

I asked God to show me some sign if Kenneth is the one for me. I asked Him to remove him from my heart if he is not. I also asked him for the strength and courage to walk away from Remo.

When I finished my prayer, I felt compelled to call my mother. I told her everything that had happened and I told her all about Kenneth. I have always been able to talk to my mother and as usual, her words were a comfort to me. I told her I needed to come home for a while. She welcomed me and promised to be at my house the following morning to help me gather up my things.

I was determined to end my nightmare before I went to sleep and lost my courage. So, I called Bam after I spoke with my mother, to get her advice about my house, the furniture and appliances that Remo bought and other potential legal issues.

165

She promised to draw up a lease agreement between Prince and me.

"Property is always a good investment and you should keep it," she advised. And, as far as the things Remo purchased and put in my house, "Gifts," she said, "he can try to take them if he wants to, but I'll take him to court!"

Before getting off the phone with Bam, she promised that she and Marilyn would come by in the morning to help me pack. As I dozed off to sleep, I felt peace, knowing that the episodes with Remo were finally over. A heavy weight had been lifted.

Chapter 27

A BEAUTIFUL DAY

*T*he next morning, I started cleaning out my closet, throwing away "trash" and other things that I did not want. When I walked outside with the trash bag, I paused and looked up into the sky. The sun was shining, the sky was clear, I felt peace. It was going to be a beautiful day.

I turned to go back inside, when Remo stepped out from behind my car. He was looking rough. He looked as if he had not slept, he had not bathed and he was wearing the same clothes from the day before.

"What are you doing here? Where is your truck?" I asked.

"The cops are after me. I've been hiding all night. I left my truck at a friend's house. I just had to talk to you."

I checked myself. I wasn't afraid anymore. I just looked at him. He was pathetic.

"I'm sorry, baby," He apologized, walking towards me.

"It's over, Remo! Don't you get it?"

"I know you're mad at me, but we can..."

"I think you'd better leave, now, Remo."

"I was going to give you a promise ring for Christmas. If you want me to, I can give it to you now," he was begging and pathetic.

"I never wanted you in the first place, Remo! I don't want any ring from you; I don't want anything from you! I don't want *YOU*!"

Seeing that I wasn't getting through to him, I turned to walk back inside. When I did, Remo pushed me! He pushed me so hard that the top of my body jerked back from the force, and then I fell forward, knees first, and slid several feet. I felt the grass burn my face as I slid, knocking my glasses off my face.

Without turning around to him, I found my glasses underneath my body. I stood up, wiped my glasses off, put them back on my face and kept walking towards my house. Remo was standing there, yelling and cursing. I just ignored him and kept walking.

About that time, I could see Prince standing in the door way. I heard a car screach to a halt behind me. I turned to see Bam's BMW come to a halt.

Things happened so fast. Remo was still yelling and cursing at me, Bam jumped out of her car, dressed to the 9's, and ran up to Remo. Remo turned just in time for his face to make connection with Bam's fist – twice! He was stunned! He stumbled back and Bam hit him again. As he went down on one knee, Bam was taking off her shoes. She started dancing around like a champion boxer, ready to land her next punch.

"C'mon here! Get up! Get cho' big fat, no good..." I could tell she wanted to cuss –not curse, but cuss! "Get up so I can knock you down again! You look real good falling!"

This was a side of Bam that I had never seen before. It was a welcomed sight!

It wasn't long beore the police pulled up. Cedric came over to us while the other cop went over to Remo, to place him under arrest. Cedric smiled at Bam and said, "Okay, Ms. Bam, we can take it from here." We all laughed with relief.

"Thanks for calling Cedric," I said to Prince as I walked towards him.

He gave me a hug and said, "I didn't call the cops"

"Well, if you didn't, who did?" I asked with an inquisitive look on my face.

"I did." I heard Patrice's voice coming from inside my house. There she was, standing in the doorway, with the cordless phone in her hand. She was wearing one of Prince's shirts.

I smiled up at Prince. He smiled back at me, nodding his head and winking his eye. He put his arm around my shoulder and we watched as the police put Remo into their vehicle. Marilyn and Bam joined us on the porch and watched with us. I looked up towards the sky again. Yes, it is going to be a beautiful day.

My friends finished helping me pack the things I wanted to take to my mother's house. The things that I could not carry, I boxed them up and put them in the garage. As we were finishing up, my mother arrived in her van.

Mother greeted everyone with hugs and kisses. She let us know that she'd brought some food with her. We all chatted while we ate fried chicken, potato salad, baked beans, dinner rolls and peach cobbler. Then we loaded as much of my things as we could into my mother's van and my car.

The day was coming to an end. I realized I had not checked my mail during the day. I went to the mail box, not expecting anything special or significant. To my surprise, there was a letter from Kenneth!

I sat down on the curb as I held the letter in my hand. I just stared at it, almost too afraid to open it. I knew what I wanted it to say, but would it contain anything in my favor? I knew that I'd just mailed my letter to Kenneth on the day before so I reasoned this letter could not be a response to the one that I'd sent him.

Carefully, I opened the letter. My hands were shaking. When I opened the seal, a hint of Kenneth's cologne escaped from the confines of the envelope. I held my breath as I unfolded the pages. My eyes filled with tears as I read the words:

Dear Niecy,

How are you? I'm sick! And I am drunk. For the first time in my life—and last time in my life—I am drunk. I have been thinking about you so much that I am sick! I tried to get you out of my mind and thought that a few beers might do the trick. I was wrong! Now, not only are you still on my mind, but I'm sitting here, with a trash can between my knees so that I can throw up. I thought I should write this letter before I loose my courage.

What can I say? I love you! I really, really love you! I can't stop thinking about you! I understand if you don't want me. I just need you to tell me so that I can get on with my life.

When you didn't come to San Antonio, I tried calling you but the phone stayed busy. I thought you were trying to avoid me. I tried to get you out of my mind then, but I couldn't. My friends thought I was crazy for planning

170

the picnic with you. I was so happy that you went with me. I thought you were happy to see me too, but when I saw you cleaning up everything, I thought you'd had enough of me! Tell me, am I wrong? Are you tired of me? I have to know. I can't eat, I can't sleep! I love you! I really, really love you!

Love always,
Kenneth Ke-Mon Williams
P.S.: Please call me or write me as soon as you get this letter. I've just got to know.

I finished reading the letter, through my tears, in the privacy of the evening, as the sun was going down. Everyone was still talking in the kitchen when I went back inside. No one seemed to notice that I was missing. My mother was keeping everyone entertained with stories of my childhood. I didn't mind. I had a very important phone call to make.

I hurried to my bedroom for privacy. My hands trembled as I quickly dialed Kenneth's number. I could hear myself breathing heavily into the phone as I waited for Kenneth to answer.

"Hello?" his smooth voice filled my ear.

"Hi, Kenneth. It's me, Niecy."

"Hey, Niecy! How are you?"

"I received your letter today."

"You did? I didn't know what happened to that letter. I must have passed out or something. I really don't remember what I wrote or anything. I think one of my friends mailed it for me. Anyway, I'm so glad you called. It's good to hear your voice."

His words were mixed. I couldn't get a feel for what he was feeling. Did he mean what he'd written or was he just writing in a drunken stupor? I didn't want to discuss it over the phone. I had to see him in person.

"I'm coming to Dallas in the morning. Is there any reason why I couldn't come by to see you?" I asked.

"You're coming to Dallas?"

"Yes, I am!"

"In the morning?"

"Yes, in the morning!" I hoped I was sensing some excitement rising up in him as we continued our conversation. Neither of us said anything on a personal note. I did not mention the letter any more. I just wanted to see him face to face.

Before we ended our phone conversation, he gave me directions to his office in Dallas. He told me to look for a big cement arch in the parking lot where his office building is located. I scratched down the vague directions and slid them into my pocket before I joined everyone else in the kitchen.

"Where did you disappear to?" my mother asked.

"I had something I needed to check in my bedroom," I responded as honestly as I could. Even though I told my mother about Kenneth, I'm sure she would not appreciate my going to Dallas first thing in the morning, so soon after ending all ties with Remo.

With the evening growing late, my mother and I left in our separate vehicles. Patrice agreed to come with me. She didn't know that I would need her to be with me when I went to Dallas in the morning.

Chapter 28

REUNITED

♥

*T*he next morning, I got up early to start on my way to Dallas. I left without telling my mother where I was going. I did not want to tell her a lie, so I chose not to tell her anything. I just left her a note telling her that Patrice and I were taking a short drive and that I needed some time to think.

Making my way to Dallas was simple enough. It was finding my way to Kenneth that was going to be the problem. I started looking at the directions that Kenneth gave me and realized how vague they were. I was trying hard not to show my anxiety, but Patrice was making me so nervous that I almost wished I'd come alone.

"How are we going to find him? Do you know how big Dallas is? Do you even know where he works? Do you even know if he's going to be at work today? He may be out of town. He may..." Patrice was rambling.

"Shut up, Patrice!" I was already nervous and I didn't need Patrice to cause my anticipation level to increase.

"Listen," I tried to explain, "I called him last night to tell him I was coming. He gave me directions, see?" I held up a piece of paper with the slightest hint of directions scribbled on it. I could barely read my own handwriting.

"He knows I'm coming!" I tried to assure Patrice and myself as well. I was trying not to concentrate on the fact that when Kenneth was giving me the directions, he was very vague. It was as if he didn't believe I was coming, or worse, he didn't want me to come. Either way, I just had to see whether or not this was the man for me.

"God," I promised myself, "if I don't get some sign today, I will go back to Austin, quit my job, join the army, and move far away from here and work to get this man out of my mind, out of my heart and out of my life forever!"

I saw a sign which indicated that my first exit was a short distance away. I followed the scribbled directions as well as I could. To be honest, I wasn't sure I was gong to find Kenneth. The directions were so incomplete. I should have pressed him for more details.

Suddenly, I heard a voice say, "turn here". I remembered how Ms. Dee said that if I believed that God would speak to me, then I would hear His voice when He did speak. I believed He was speaking to me, so I turned. A few blocks later, the inner voie said again, "turn here". For a brief moment, I thought I was lost. Then, I heard Patrice scream. I looked up and saw point her finger further down the street.

"There's the arch, there's the arch!" she yelled and pointed.

I felt my excitement increasing. I pulled into the large parking lot and began the diligent search for a place to park.

"How are you going to find him? This building is so huge," Patrice stated with a bit of panic in her voice.

"I'm going to stop the first brother I see in a suit and ask him if he knows Kenneth," I responded with confidence.

"Oh, so that's your plan," Patrie responded as she threw up her hands in defeat and fell back into her seat. I finished pulling my car into the parking space near the front of the entrance into the building.

"I have faith, Patrice. Today, I will know whether or not this man is the man for me. Now, come on!"

I stepped out of my car and onto the side walk. The very first person I saw was a young African American male, wearing a navy business suit, headed into the building.

"Excuse me." The young man stopped and waited for me to catch up with him.

"Do you know where I can find Kenneth Williams? I'm supposed to be meeting him..."

Before I could finish my question, the young man's attention was on my face. As a look of revelation spread across his face, he smiled, pointed at me and said, almost screaming, "You're Niecy! I mean, Angela Denise West!" He looked more excited than I did.

"Yes, I am," I responded, wondering how he knew my name, my whole name.

He grabbed my hand and continued talking.

"I know exactly where Kenneth is. I'm taking you directly to him because I don't want you to get lost. Did you get my letter? I mean Kenneth's letter that I mailed to you for him?"

He was walking and talking so fast, Patrice and I were almost running trying to keep up! We passed the receptionist's desk.

"This is Angela!" He shouted to the clerk, as he was pointing at me. Now, I was really confused.

The receptionist asked, "Who?"

"Kenneth's Angela! You know! Niecy!" He responded as he continued to hold on to my hand and we continued our quest to locate Kenneth.

"Niecy?" I could see she was thinking. Then, as if a light clicked on, she put her hands over her mouth as if she was trying to contain a scream.

"Ooo, I've got to call..." her voice trailed off in the distance. We were too far away for me to hear who it was she was going to call.

We paused at the elevator. My heart was pounding almost out of my chest. My mind was racing, trying to put all of this together. I wanted to start jumping up and down, not like a two year old having a tantrum, but like a poor man who just won a multi-million dollar lottery. I strained to keep the smile from creeping up on my face. I didn't want to be too presumptuous.

The elevator opened. Another young man was about to step out. My escort, who still had me by the hand said to him, "This is Angela!" proudly pointing at me again.

"From Austin?" the guy asked as we stepped into the elevator.

"Yeah! I'm taking her to Kenneth right now!"

The elevator door was about to close when the second man interfered with the door.

"I'm going with you! I don't want to miss this." he said.

My escort finally introduced himself, "I'm Steve and this is Chad." he said, pointing to himself and then to Chad. We all said our "hello's" while the elevatory continued its climb. Everyone else in the elevator was consumed with their conversation while my mind was working over time trying to put all of the pieces to this newly developing puzzle together.

The elevator doors opened and revealed an open-office floor plan. There were desk neatly arranged with separating cubicles, copy machines and other work stations all scattered throughout the area. I was scanning the faces of the busy employees, looking for that one special, familiar face.

"Hey, everybody!" Steve called out to get everyone's attention. "This is Angela!"

Immediately, the workers who'd stopped in their tracks to hear Steve's announcement, became engaged in a buzz of conversation, as Steve led me through the work stations, I could hear things like:

"All right!"

"It's about time."

"This is great."

"It's so romantic."

"We finally get to meet her!"

"She is cute."

"This is exciting!"

"Is this Angela from Austin?"

"Does Kenneth know she's made it?

Suddenly, Steve paused and pointed towards one of the offices that lined the outside wall of the office space.

"Look," he said.

I followed the direction of his pointing finger. There, standing in the doorway of one of the offices, was Kenneth. The look on his face was a mixture of confusion, shock, and excitement, all in one. Our eyes met. Without a word or change in his expression, he darted back into his office. I was confused.

"He doesn't want to see me," I said half to Steve and half to myself. I could feel hot tears swelling up in my eyes and a huge lump growing in my throat. I turned back towards the elevator, looking for a quick exit. I couldn't go anywhere! My way was blocked by the crowd that was still growing behind me.

Steve tapped me on my shoulder. When I turned to acknowledge him, he pointed again. I looked. Kenneth was walking towards me. There was a smile on his face that I had not seen before. He walked up to me and took both my hands in his.

"I can hardly believe you're here…I mean…I've dreamed for so long…I've prayed… I just want…" He could

177

hardly speak. He paused and took a deep breath. I felt his hands shaking. He was just as nervous as I was.

"I…I…" I tried to tell him that I love him.

But, before I could get the words out, he put his finger gently on my lips and said, "Me first. I have waited a long time for this."

With that being said, he went down on one knee, still with both my hands enclosed in his. He reached into his pocket and pulled out a little black box. As he was opening the box and staring into my eyes, he asked, "Angela Denise West, will you marry me?"

The silence in the office was deafening. I could hear the clock on the wall ticking, an airplane over head, and the water cooler gurgling. I could feel the tears rolling down my face.

"Yes…yes, I will marry you," I whispered. I could hardly get my response out before the whole office broke out in a thunderous applause and cheer.

Kenneth rose from his knee and put the engagement ring on my finger. We shared a kiss and the crowd continued to applaud and cheer to show their approval.

After the noise settled, some of the employees returned to their desk while others congratulated us both. Several of them said, "We've heard so much about you."

"He talks about you all the time."

"You are one lucky lady."

"Kenneth is lucky to have a lady like you."

"He didn't think you were coming."

"Kenny really loves you."

"It's good to finally meet you!"

As things were getting back to normal, I realized Patrice was preoccupied, talking to Steve. Kenneth took me by the hand and escorted me into his office. What I saw next, made me laugh and cry all at the same time. As I looked around his office, I saw every picture I'd sent him over the last seven years, framed and displayed in his office! He even had a poem that I'd written to him professionally reprinted, framed and hanging on his wall.

"I love you so much!" He finally said.

I reached up to hug him and he returned my embrace. As he leaned down to kiss me, he closed the door to his office behind us, to keep the staring eyes of the more romantic office employees from seeing too much.

I shouted to myself, "Thank you, God! I have found my perfect man."

A word from *my* "perfect" man,
We hope you have enjoyed reading "Waiting for the Perfect Man"!
Based on the request from readers who have enjoyed this book before
you, the writer has developed this book into a series. The writer also
has other books and ministry tapes available. To be made aware of
upcoming releases and other products, please complete form below to
be added to our mail list. We look forward to hearing from you!

Sincerely,
Garland K. Z. Flakes

The next books will be published in this order:

Waiting for the Perfect Man: Patrice's Story

Waiting for the Perfect Man: Marilyn's Story

Waiting for the Perfect Man: Beverly's Story (Ms. BAM)

Waiting for the Perfect Man: Ms. Dee's Story

Waiting for the Perfect Man: KiKi's Story

Mail to: Delena K. Flakes
PO Box 13058
Beaumont, TX 77726-3058

Name: _____

Address: _____

City & State: _____

Zip: _____Email:_____

www.ingramcontent.com/pod-product-compliance
Lightning Source LLC
Chambersburg PA
CBHW031319120626
46554CB00001BA/472